CALROD

CONDEMNED

AVA BENTON

1

———

Calrod

I was going to get stuck under this damn kitchen sink if I wasn't careful. I'd been lying here for ten minutes trying in vain to figure out where the leak was coming from. Didn't help half that time, I was too distracted to pay much attention to what I was supposed to be working on. Life had drastically changed in the last year. Not that I was complaining about it. Not really.

Arkon and Jasmine were together and on the verge of having a baby. Dagon even found his mate and had moved back to Oak Hollow with her. We were turning into one big happy family.

They were, at least. I wasn't sure I could ever have

what they did. I twisted the wrench, grunting with the effort to loosen the fitting. It wasn't that I didn't want to be happy. I just didn't deserve it, not after what I'd done.

Flashes of a grinning face right before I was betrayed rose in my mind. I growled, and that face was replaced by a different one. One that had made my heart stutter and my blood burn. The dark underside of the sink drifted away, and I was taken back to the day that woman fell right into me at the antique store...

After checking the perimeter around the antique shop, I headed inside to tell Arkon it was safe. He'd been out of his mind since I showed up with that damn picture of Dagon's sketch. I never should've shown it to him, but I had only ever lied to my brother about one thing. That lie was enough to damn me for eternity as far as I was concerned. Lying to him about anything else just didn't seem fair.

I entered the shop, ready to find Arkon. His voice came from the backroom, and I started in that direction. A curse came from my left, and I spotted a woman atop a stepladder. She was talking to herself while she tried to fix a painting that was hanging crooked. It was impossible not to notice her curves or the way her ass looked in those damn jeans she had on. My gaze drifted lower, and I frowned.

She was barefoot. On a ladder. How was that a good idea?

"Will you stop it," she snapped, exasperated. The frame she'd just righted slanted to the right again. She grunted, tilting it back the other way. She leaned away from the wall, shoving curly black hair from her face. She crossed her arms, glowering at the painting. A rush of cold air blew past me, and the picture went right back to being crooked. "Damn it. I've had enough of you today." She reached over to correct it a third time, but the ladder shifted beneath her. She cursed, lost her balance, and I rushed forward.

She collided with me, and we hit the floor with several curses and a loud thud. I ended up with a mouth full of hair until the woman sat upright, her legs slipping to either side of my body. "Shit, sorry! I'm sorry, are you okay? Holy shit, you moved fast," she rambled.

I started to reply, but a pair of shimmering hazel eyes full of life so intense made me lose focus. The warmth of her body pressed intimately against mine had me fighting the urge to grab her hip with one hand and bury the other in her hair while I kissed her. Those eyes narrowed slightly, but her lips curled into an admiring grin of her own.

"You're Calrod," she said and held out her hand. "Jasmine mentioned something about you being in town. I'm Cara."

I blinked, finally able to break my gaze from hers, and glanced at her hand. I took it, mine engulfing hers. The same burst of warmth I already experienced from her body shocked me a second time. She studied our joined hands curiously, too, as if she felt the same thing.

"Nice to meet you." I was still shaking her hand when her eyes widened, and she scurried to get off me.

"Sorry, I wasn't even thinking," she said, her cheeks burning bright red. "I uh, sorry about that. I mean landing on you and, you know, straddling you. I usually don't do that shit when I first meet someone."

"I've had worst first impressions." I got to my feet. "Maybe you shouldn't be up there by yourself."

"Yeah, well, had to fix a painting, and I'm pretty sure Jas and Arkon are necking in the backroom," she said, laughing. "They're like teenagers with how much they make out." She shifted her eyes to the wall and sighed. "And the painting is still crooked. That's awesome."

She started for the ladder, but I held out my hand. "Why don't you let me do that?"

I climbed up and fixed the painting, not giving her a chance to argue. I adjusted the picture on the nail and stepped back down. She had her arms crossed, and I was sure I heard her whisper, "Figures, you damn traitors," under her breath.

"What was that?"

"Hmm? Oh, nothing. You must have a magic touch or something."

"Or something," I said, unable to stop looking at her. Each time, I caught a new detail, how the light played off her black hair or how her toenails were painted sea blue, matching her fingernails. Or the freckles barely noticeable on her cheeks. The air shifted around me, and my heart pounded. Breathing became a challenge, and my inner fire whispered the only word that could doom me.

Mine.

"Calrod?"

"Sorry, I should find Arkon," I mumbled, backing away.

"Yeah, course. I guess I'll see you around. You staying in Oak Hollow long?"

"No plans to leave," I replied, unsure where that even came from, but damn if it didn't make her eyes light up. I gave her a brief smile and walked off as fast as I could.

Mine. Cara was mine, but gods, I couldn't let myself have her...

Forgetting to keep my demonic strength in check, I pulled the wrench too hard to the right, yanking the pipe clear of the fitting. Water sputtered out, and I cursed, fighting against the spray. I was sure I'd shut the water off before I crawled down here to start working.

In the kitchen came a curse followed by rushing steps. "Shit, hang on!"

I was too busy getting sprayed in the face with water to reply. Eventually, the stream ebbed, and I shimmied out from under the sink, drenched, and wiping water out of my eyes. The air in the room changed, and I gritted my teeth, reminding myself not to give in to what my inner fire whispered every time I was near her.

A towel landed in my lap. I glanced up at the beer that appeared in front of my face next. The hand holding it had nails painted a dark green with a swirling black pattern on them. Several silver bands decorated her fingers, and matching bangles clinked on her wrist.

"Sorry about that," Cara Night said, cringing and still holding out the beer. "You could've waited 'til I got home to start on it. I thought I told you where the shut-off valve was."

"You did," I replied, taking the beer with a grunt of thanks. I stood up, draping the damp towel over the edge of the sink behind me. "Guess I didn't turn it off all the way. And I thought you were working late today."

"Was, but Jasmine decided to close up early and told me to go home, too."

From across her tiny kitchen, her hazel eyes studied me. That inquisitive look always made me wonder what she was thinking, what she was seeing when she looked at me. My glamour was firmly in place, so she wasn't seeing the real me. Yet every time she got that look in her eyes, I felt exposed. Like she could see all of me, and not just what was on the surface. If I was candid with myself, I was damn jealous Arkon and Dagon could be themselves as much as they were. I was still hiding. How could I not be? No matter what instinct told me when it came to Cara, it wasn't possible.

I wouldn't let it be possible.

I cleared my throat, casually glancing around the tiny kitchen. Cara lived in a cottage at the edge of town. Though it wasn't falling apart like Jasmine's farmhouse had been, it still needed some repairs every now and then to maintain the old place. Ever since I settled down here to stay close to Arkon—at least I told myself it was only for his sake—I started picking up odd jobs as a handyman around town. Now, I had become the local person everyone called for repairs. I'd come over to fix a few outlets at Cara's place, then ended up seeing more minor things that could stand to be updated.

And if I wasn't finding them, she was texting me saying something else was broken. I knew what was going on here, but as much as I enjoyed our back-and-forth game, it couldn't go anywhere. One of these days, I'd have to let her know that. I had to stop playing and let her move on with her life.

"You alright?" Cara asked, peering at me over her beer bottle.

It was impossible not to watch her lips while she took a long sip or how she licked them afterward. She had on a snug pair of bootcut jeans and a green tank top that matched her nails. Her curly, black hair was pulled back in a black cloth tie, showing off the gentle curves of her face. My lips twitched into a brief smile at the light dusting of freckles on her cheeks. Just like every time I saw her, those eyes were so bright and full of life, like she was ready to burst out laughing at any given second. She set her beer down with a quiet thud on the oak kitchen table, and her brow arched.

"Calrod? Did I lose you somewhere?"

"Huh?" I murmured, then coughed. "Sorry, just

ah, long day. And that damn sink of yours is a nightmare."

"Why I called you." Her eyes darted down my body then, away, her smile making my heart beat a little faster. She went to the fridge and pulled it open. "You eaten yet tonight? I can make you dinner."

"For what?"

"Can't a woman just offer a man some food? You did just get drenched by my sink." She bent over, and my hand closed around the edge of the counter. I swallowed back a curse at how the jeans showed off her ass. "You want it or what?"

"What?" I blurted.

She straightened, a smile playing across her lips. "Food, Calrod. That thing you have to eat to sustain life." She laughed warmly. "Man, you really are having an off day. You didn't have to come over tonight, you know."

"You've been complaining about that sink for weeks."

"Not to you."

"No, but to Jas, and she tells Arkon, who's kind enough to pass it along to me."

She crossed her arms, cocking her hip to rest against the counter. "I think you need to stop being so nice. When was the last time you took a day off? Every time I see you, you're running around town trying to fix something for everyone else."

I shrugged. "I don't have anything else to do."

"Don't you want a life that doesn't involve leaky pipes and broken fences?"

"I like keeping busy."

"There are plenty of other ways to keep busy."

She sidled closer, her hips swaying without her even trying. I knew because I'd watched her at the antique store plenty of times, off in her own little world. She had a natural grace in how she moved. It was one of the reasons I'd been drawn to her in the first place. The other was that damn laugh of hers. I might be able to play with fire, but I'd never felt like I was burning like a wildfire until the first time she laughed in front of me. That was unbridled heat, and I hadn't been able to get enough of it. I'd told myself I could handle being near her, especially if she didn't care about me as I'd started to do for her.

Then one day, I'd come by the store to fix a few lights for Jasmine, and Cara had been there instead. We'd ended up talking most of the day, only stopping if a customer had entered the shop. I'd stayed until closing without even realizing it. When I'd gone home that night, I hadn't been able to stop grinning. I might not have shared the full details of my life with Cara, but simply listening to her tell me the local ghost folklore surrounding the town had been more than enough. She was so animated when she got really excited, bouncing on the balls of her feet with her hands moving every which way. She'd talk so fast sometimes, I had to make her repeat herself. It was like she was hyped on caffeine without having a bit to drink.

But the wonder I'd had with being able to speak with someone so naturally hadn't lasted. It couldn't. The last time I'd opened my heart to a woman, she'd done far worse than just crush it.

Cara was a couple of feet away, nibbling her lip, and I was frozen on what I should do. This wasn't the first time the tension had risen to lung-crushing heights between us. I'd lost count of how many times our hands brushed, or she'd bump into me if we were at the shop together or at the farmhouse. I was convinced Jasmine was purposely creating situations for Cara and me to be alone. Telling her to stop would mean explaining why I didn't want to give in to what I felt for Cara. Not even my brothers knew, and they weren't going to. It was my burden to carry for the rest of my life.

My guilt to deal with. Besides, if I gave in, I'd only ruin her life in the end.

She inched closer. I made the mistake of breathing in deeply through my nose. Instantly, my body relaxed at the familiar fragrance that was all her. She always had an earthy scent about her, not dirt exactly, but it reminded me of the forest during a soft rain. There was the slightest hint of leather and old books, too. That came from all the work she did at the antique store. A growl started to rumble through my chest, but I forced myself to stop the second Cara tilted her head as if hearing it.

Keeping my demon side hidden around her was becoming a challenge. But the more time I spent around her, or simply in the shop when she was there, I was starting to realize I wasn't the only one with secrets. There were times she looked off at nothing. She'd jump whenever someone called her name, almost as if she hadn't been mentally present at all. Or she'd be whispering to herself in a corner. She was often jittery and on edge, but there was never an easy explanation as to why. Once again lost in my musings of what Cara could possibly be hiding, I hadn't noticed how much nearer she'd moved toward me. It wouldn't take much for me to reach out and drag her to me.

"There's something I've been wanting to ask you," she said.

"Yeah?" I asked, the word coming out rough.

Her eyes glimmered. "Yeah." She took a deep breath, let it out, and started to speak, but my cell going off interrupted her. I ignored it, too transfixed by her lips and how much of an idiot I was right then to answer it. "Calrod."

"Hmm?"

"Your phone?"

It stopped ringing, and I didn't bother reaching for it. My mind had started picturing what it'd be like to give in and kiss Cara. Just once. Maybe I was wrong about my feelings for her. I could find out and end this obsession with her tonight.

Or make it a hundred times worse.

My cell went off again, and I continued to ignore it. Cara was barely a breath away from touching me now. If I breathed any faster, our bodies would meet. I was still clutching the beer in my hand. Without letting her eyes leave mine, she took it from me and set it aside. This close, she had to tilt her head back to keep looking at me. Her scent continued to surround me, then she chuckled.

"You smell like a woodshop and sink water," she mused.

"That second part is your fault." I told myself to push her away, but my hands refused to listen to me. "You uh, said you had something to ask me?"

"Did I? Don't remember now."

The kitchen hadn't been this warm before. It couldn't have been. An errant spark of fire ignited under my palm, and I quickly snuffed it out. That was the last thing Cara needed to see, me summoning fire in her kitchen. She raised up on her toes, her eyes slipping to my lips, then her house phone rang. Rolling her eyes, she backed away and snatched the cordless off the counter.

"Hello?" Her brow furrowed. "Hey, Arkon. Yeah, he's here. Jas okay?" There was a pause, then she let out a sigh of relief. "Good, yeah, hang on." She held out the phone to me. "Your brother, and he doesn't sound very happy."

I took the phone, asking, "What's wrong?"

"You need to get to the farmhouse now," Arkon snapped.

"Care to tell me why?"

"Not over the phone. Dagon and Morgan are here."

"What's going on?" I asked, the moment I almost had with Cara fading out of existence.

"Carridan," Arkon said, and my usually warm body froze.

"I'll be there soon as I can." I hung up and handed the phone back to Cara. "I have to go."

"Everything okay?"

"Sort of." There was no easy way to explain, and I wasn't about to leave her with a heap of lies I might not remember well enough to keep straight. I turned around, cursing at the sight of the sink. "I'll fix the pipe the best I can, then come back later and fix it. I'm sorry."

"Don't worry about it. If you need to go, just go."

"Cara," I started, but she grabbed my hand, then shoved me out of the kitchen and through the living room.

"I'm pretty handy when I need to be. Go. I just hope everything's okay."

It wasn't, but I said I was sure it would be and set off without a backward glance. I climbed into the old two-door red truck I used while on the job and pulled out of the drive. Cara was still at the front door, a worried frown on her face.

I waved, then sped out of town. I reached the farmhouse in record time, parking beside Dagon's vehicle. I ran to the house, bursting through the front door. Arkon was pacing from the kitchen to the living room and back, his eye twitching and his hands flexing nonstop at his sides. Jasmine stood with Morgan by the fireplace, and Dagon was on the couch, holding his head in his hands.

"Well?" I growled, and everyone turned to me.

"We have a problem," Dagon said, not lifting his head even after I came around the couch.

I dropped the glamour I'd had in place all day, then moved to stop Arkon from walking around. He snarled, shoving at me, but I gripped his shoulders hard and shook him. "You said Carridan. Is he here?"

Arkon's eyes shimmered dark amber. "Ask our brother."

"You going to be alright?"

Arkon pushed me again. This time, I let him, and he looked to Jasmine. "I can't do this," he whispered. "If he's coming here, I can't lose you or the baby. I should've killed him. I should've gone through the damn veil months ago and—"

"And what?" Jasmine interrupted hotly. "Died before we could even be together? Before we could start a family?" She stormed to him, holding his face firmly in her hands. "Don't start that shit. Nothing is going to happen to me, or the baby, or you for that matter. You blaming yourself isn't going to help anybody."

He tried to tear himself away from her, but she snatched his hands and planted them on her pregnant belly. His face softened, and he sank to his knees, pressing his cheek to where their unborn child waited for them.

"If Carridan is coming to Oak Hollow, you can't go losing your shit," Jasmine ordered. "Got it?"

He nodded, but she snapped his full name, and he looked up at her. "I promise I won't go off on my own to try and kill him."

"Good." She pulled him to his feet and kissed him fiercely.

I backed away, giving them space, and returned to Dagon on the couch. "Tell me exactly what you saw," I said, and he finally looked up. His eyes were wide with panic. Morgan hurried to him, squeezing his hand while she sat on the armrest next to his right. "Dagon."

"Right, sorry." He blinked rapidly, then cleared his throat. "I saw Prince Carridan walking on a gravel road surrounded by woods. He wasn't alone, and there was something weird about him. He felt off. No other princes, far as I could see."

"You sure it was in Oak Hollow?" I asked.

Dagon held up his hands, then let them fall to the couch cushions. "Why else would I see that shit?"

Even if it wasn't here, being prepared for Carridan's arrival was something we should've done the second we all ended up here. "Time frame?"

He shrugged. "Summer? Trees hadn't started turning yet. The vision was so damn fast."

It was barely June. Summer didn't narrow down his arrival much at all. He could show up tomorrow or a year from now. I kept my face blank and attempted not to let my thoughts get too carried away in case Dagon decided to take a peek inside my head.

"Did you contact Cyrene yet?" I asked.

"Wanted to fill you in first." Dagon leaned back against the cushions. "What do we do? Leave?"

"No," Jasmine snapped.

Arkon growled.

She glared at him. "Don't even start with me. We're not giving up our home. If he found us once, then he can find us again. I'm not leaving."

Arkon's lips thinned, but to my surprise, he didn't argue. "Then you better be willing to do everything I tell you from this point forward. Everything, Jas. I'm not putting you or the baby at risk."

"Do whatever you have to do as long as we stay here, and we stay together," she said, turning to gaze pointedly at Dagon then me.

Why was she giving me that look? She didn't know the truth because Arkon didn't know. Sensing another pair of eyes on me, I turned and inwardly cursed. Having Dagon around reading minds was bad enough. I had yet to remember Morgan's ability to read energies and emotions. From the worry coursing through her eyes right then, she was picking up on way too much from me.

"Dagon, contact Cyrene," Arkon said. "We need her here tonight. The warding around the house needs to be increased. And around the damn shop, too."

"Why not put it up all around town?" Dagon suggested.

"Can we do that?" Jasmine asked.

"I don't see why the hell not. Give us a chance to be warned of his arrival if nothing else," Arkon replied. "And you, my psychotic lover, are not to be alone. Ever. I want to hear you say it right now in front of all these witnesses. You do not go anywhere alone, not even home."

Jasmine's face scrunched, but she let out a sigh,

giving in. "I promise I won't go anywhere alone, not even home."

"Good. One of us is to be with you at all times. No exceptions."

Jasmine's lips twitched. "Even in the shower?"

"Jas." Arkon's answering grumble while he drew her into his arms for a heated kiss that had me turning away was answer enough.

"What?" she murmured. "Just trying to lighten the mood."

I didn't blame Arkon for his concerns. Jasmine was the most vulnerable out of all of us. If Carridan learned she was pregnant with Arkon's child, he'd use her against him in the worst way possible. The bastard would probably try to steal their baby. Arkon had watched her die once already. If he had to go through that a second time and lose that precious life growing inside her, there'd be no coming back for my brother.

Morgan and Dagon were whispering to each other, then he dragged her onto his arms, hugging her. As happy as I was for my brothers, seeing them like this was precisely why I couldn't get close to the one person I wanted to. What was the point when I might be dead in a few months?

The last thing Carridan needed was more

leverage to use against any of us. Morgan had proved how powerful she was, more so with Dagon at her side. And though we hadn't seen it yet, Cyrene swore up and down Jasmine had magic running through her veins that we'd all get to see soon enough. Arkon had grilled Cyrene about that notion several times. She'd finally confessed she'd lied back when he first asked her about Jasmine and the dagger known as Soul Piercer. Cyrene hadn't wanted Arkon to use the blade because of something else she'd seen. What that might be, we remained unsure of. Cyrene was too damn good at keeping secrets.

Far as I knew, Cara was full mortal. The farther away she stayed from me, the better. She'd still be coming into the shop for work, but as long as she went home alone every night, she'd be safe. I'd make sure of it.

I wandered out onto the front porch, staring up at the stars blinking away in the sky. We'd been running on luck for years. Figures now was when it'd run out. The screen door opened behind me, and Dagon and Zach appeared at the railing on either side of me.

"If he comes here, it's going to get messy," I warned. "You sure you don't want to take Jasmine away? Go into hiding somewhere else?"

"And have her hate me for years?" Arkon barked a laugh. "She's right. If we run, Carridan can always find us again. If he's coming to Oak Hollow, he knows we're alive."

"How's what I want to know," Dagon muttered.

"Doesn't matter anymore. He knows, and he's coming for us. We have to be ready for him. This time, he doesn't get to walk away with his head attached to his body." My hands curled around the railing until it creaked from the pressure.

"If we kill a prince, the entire Underworld might rise against us," Dagon whispered.

"They've been manipulated by him for years," Arkon said. "Might be grateful instead."

"Fifty-fifty chance," I added, and we exchanged a serious look. "If it comes down to one of us dealing the final blow, I'll do it. The blame can be laid at my feet, and you two can get on with your lives."

"You think we're going to let them take you? Why would we do that?" Dagon snapped.

I sensed him starting to poke around in my thoughts and growled in warning, tucking those horrible memories further out of reach. "Don't argue with me. I'm the eldest, and I'll do whatever has to be done to save you both. You have families to look after now. End of discussion."

"Calrod," Arkon argued, but I stormed away from him, down the porch steps, and across the drive.

"Call Cyrene. I'm going to check the perimeter," I yelled over my shoulder.

Alone in the darkness of the forest, my shoulders sagged, and I buried my claws into the trunk of a nearby tree. I'd sworn I would take my secret with me to the grave. That was turning out to be far sooner than I assumed, but it was for the best.

My brothers never needed to know I was the reason we were in this mess to begin with.

That I was the reason our parents were murdered, and our lives were thrown into chaos.

2

Cara

Jasmine's curses from the storeroom were quickly followed by a minor crash. I rushed back there and laughed. She was glaring at a broken vase at her feet.

"You know there's this thing called asking for help."

She scowled, rubbing her hands over her pregnant stomach. "I'm not that helpless."

"That big ole belly of yours would say otherwise."

"It's not that big," she mumbled with a pout.

I went for the dustpan and broom we kept hanging on the wall nearby. "I never said it was a bad thing. You pregnant is ridiculously adorable. If Arkon were here, I'm sure he'd agree with me."

"Oh, he would," Dagon said, appearing in the doorway. He was smiling, but it did nothing to chase the storm cloud of worry in his eyes. "They can't keep their damn hands to themselves anymore. He'd also be scolding you for trying to do shit you're not supposed to. Lucky it's me instead. Why don't you sit down? Rest for a bit?"

"So I can go stir crazy? No thanks," Jasmine argued and tried to take the broom from me. I held it out of reach, and she grunted. "Come on. I made the mess. At least let me clean it up."

"Dagon, go get her a cookie or something," I said.

Jasmine looked ready to strangle me.

"Remember, you love me," I said, giving her the biggest grin I could manage.

"Not my only employee anymore," she reminded me.

"Is that a threat?" I said through my cackling.

"Maybe. No." She sighed, her shoulders sagging. "I'm sorry, I'm not used to being like this." She waved at herself, then went to sit on the couch.

"Well, you couldn't have picked a better time to hire more help." I swept up the broken vase, told Jasmine to take it easy for a while in the backroom, and I'd take care of the front of the shop. She held out her hand, and I took it, giving it a squeeze. "You sure everything else is okay with you and the baby?"

"In perfect health," she assured me.

"I just can't believe you're this big," I whispered, and she smirked. "Sorry, that came out wrong."

"It's fine. We can't believe it either. Arkon's losing his mind every other day realizing how close my due date is."

"You really didn't know you were pregnant for that long?"

She shrugged, avoiding my glance. "They told me it happens. I didn't have any of the usual morning sickness or whatever. And it's my first baby so I can look normal one day, then bam! Hello, pregnant belly. So they say."

Dagon stepped into view, holding a bag of cookies from the Backroad Bakery. He must've picked them up this morning on his way to the shop. "I'll even let this count as your lunch in case Arkon asks," he said after she hesitated to take them.

I laughed and left them to finish sorting through the crate of new items behind the front counter. I shut the door on my way out, doing my best to hide my worry until I was out of sight. The day Jasmine announced she and Arkon were having a baby, I'd been surprised but extremely happy for them. I hadn't ever seen her so full of life. Arkon was good for her, and I had no doubts at all about his being there for her. What had shocked me was how fast her belly grew. She was due in less than two months, which was insane, considering when she found out she was pregnant. Shaking my head, I went back to the crates, removing a collection of old, leather-bound books with the titles mostly worn off. Care-fully, I flipped through the first few pages, making notes while glancing at the backroom every few seconds.

Jasmine might say nothing was wrong, but she was lying. For the last two weeks, if Arkon wasn't at the shop with her, then one of his brothers was. When I asked, they said it was simply because Arkon had to put finishing touches on the nursery at home and sent one of his brothers to help at the shop. It was strange, though. Calrod and Dagon were the local handymen now. It would've made more sense that they do work on the farmhouse. I tried not to go there, but it was like they were afraid to leave Jasmine alone, even with Morgan or me.

Annoyed, I set the books down heavily on the counter, wincing at the thud echoing around the shop. Morgan was great and very intuitive when it came to the items in the shop. But she was in on whatever secret they kept from me. Because that was exactly what was happening. I usually wasn't one to pry, but if Jasmine's health were at risk, or the baby's, why wouldn't they tell me? I was quite capable of watching over her while she was at work. Hell, if it was that bad, her doctor should've restricted her to bed rest. Arkon should know better than to let Jasmine keep coming to work if that was the case.

The bells above the door tinkled, and I forced my smile to stay up at the sight of a couple coming to shop instead of the man I'd hoped would swing by today.

"Doesn't matter," I mumbled to the stack of books. "Not like it's going to go anywhere. Besides, you're supposed to be worried about your friend right now. Not Calrod."

A pair of sad, blue eyes appeared in my mind's eye all the same. They weren't just ordinary blue. No, these reminded me of the sky right before night closed in. Somedays, they were so dark they were almost black. His raven hair was usually a mess, but it suited him.

And did he always have to wear such tight t-shirts and those jeans?

I tapped my fingers on the counter, remembering

how he'd looked in my kitchen a couple weeks back, drenched with sink water, and couldn't have cared less. I chuckled, wondering how much of a fool I was when it came to Calrod. After the first time I saw him, I hadn't been able to get his face out of my head or how he made whatever room he was in feel so warm. A few times, I was sure I'd caught a shimmer passing through his eyes, a shimmer made of blue flames.

"Reading too many books lately. Eyes don't shimmer with blue fire."

Pushing the stack of leatherbound volumes aside with a description of what they were tucked in the front cover, I bent down to the crates again. I removed a two-foot-tall oval painting with a letter attached to it. Curious, I unfolded the yellowed page.

"Haunted painting, huh? Interesting. Where did you come from?"

Usually, this type of gem would make my day, but my thoughts drifted right back to Calrod halfway through the letter. Despite the smile he wore, nothing seemed to chase the sorrow from his gaze. I'd asked Jasmine once or twice if something tragic happened to Calrod. She'd said nothing had, but no one walked around looking that sad for the hell of it.

Whenever I spoke with Calrod, he never told me anything about his life before showing up in Oak Hollow. I'd been wondering why he chose this small town of all places to settle down. Arkon was here, but not many brothers picked up and left everything behind simply because of a sibling. Then Dagon moved to town with his girlfriend? It was an odd place to start a handyman business, especially after hearing what Dagon's degree was in, and Morgan's for that matter. Something hinky was going on with them. This wasn't the first time I'd noticed them acting strange. Hiding things. Keeping secrets.

"So why do you want to be with him then?" I asked myself quietly. "Secrets can be dangerous."

I had a secret or two of my own I hadn't felt inclined to share with anyone.

Then again, my secret didn't revolve around the growling I'd heard coming from Calrod or his brothers on occasion. Or when I'd glance over at Arkon and thought I was looking at an entirely different person. Or those string of days when Jasmine had randomly decided to close down the shop. She'd said she was sick, but there was more going on with the two of them. They had secrets, alright. I just hoped for Jasmine's sake they weren't about her or the baby.

The couple who'd come in waved me down. Putting on my brightest smile, I left the counter and went to assist them. By the time I wrapped up and boxed the three antique statuettes, tagged a painting and the small table they purchased, Jasmine had emerged from the back. Dagon helped the couple get the items to their vehicle, and I returned to the counter and the crate of things Jasmine was currently studying with a severe look of concentration.

"I'll lay everything out on the counter for you," I said.

"Thanks. I'm sorry you're having to pick up my slack right now."

"Because I totally mind," I teased, spreading out the remaining items around her, so she didn't have to worry about bending over.

"Oh, nice. Haunted painting." She picked up the oval frame holding an oil painting of a house on a hill surrounded by an orchard. "Think it's real?"

I was going to say no, but a cool hand touched my shoulder. I glanced to my right, spotting the translucent form of a man holding a cane and wearing a top hat. He tipped it to me with a grin, then sailed around the shop that would be his home for a while.

"Definitely haunted," I murmured. The ghostly figure shimmered out of sight, but I sensed him hanging around. It was like static electricity in the air when spirits were present.

"If you say so." Jasmine carefully wiped down the wooden frame with a polishing rag. "Gorgeous piece. How are you not all over this right now?"

"What do you mean?"

"Any other day, you would've been chomping at the bit to tell me about this. And already on the computer doing research on its history." She nudged me with her elbow. "You sure you're okay?"

"Why wouldn't I be?"

"I don't know. Might have something to do with a certain handyman."

My cheeks burned, and I bent down to rummage through the crate. I settled on an intriguing box and picked it up. When I straightened, Jasmine was giving me a grin I'd learned not to like. "What?"

"Seriously? I'm pregnant, not blind."

"And?"

"And I know Calrod and you have been exchanging googly-eyed looks. How many times has he gone to your place to fix things?" She leaned in, whispering, "Things I know for a fact don't need to be fixed."

Damn. And here I thought I was sneaky with everything I'd broken so I had a reason for Calrod to swing by. The other night, I'd been close to making that first move, then Arkon had called, and I was starting to think we weren't going to get that chance again. Calrod hadn't been to my house since. I set the wooden box with a metal inset hard on the counter. "No idea what you're talking about."

"Oh, yes. Yes, you do."

"For the record, my sink actually was leaking."

"Uh-huh, sure it was. Why don't you just ask Calrod out already?"

A nervous laugh escaped me, and I tried to cover it up with a cough. "Don't meddle. You're pregnant. You should be thinking about you, not me."

"You're my best friend. I have to think about you. And both of you are pretty much family to me. I want you to be happy."

"Who says I'd be happy with him? He could turn out to be an asshole."

"Calrod? Yeah, no, not even close. He's a good guy, trust me." She gave me another playful nudge. "I wouldn't try to set you up with someone I didn't believe was good enough for you."

"It's not weird that he's your boyfriend's brother?"

"Doesn't bother me at all," she said, smiling. "That mean you're going to do it?"

I fiddled with a few loose postcards from the 1940s, also haunted. A couple of ladies wearing dresses from that era joined the ghost wearing the top hat who'd appeared once again. Great. The shop was about to be crowded, not something I wanted to deal with right now. Grunting, I leaned over and rested my forehead on the counter.

"I don't know. He acts like he's interested one second, then the next, he's hesitating. I can see the argument in his eyes, and I don't know. Pushing feels wrong."

Jasmine gave me a consoling pat on the back. "Then don't push. Just ask him out. He has to decide then what to do. Either way, you'll get an answer."

That was the problem. What if he said no? What if this whole time I'd been reading the signs wrong? I'd dated off and on since dumping my ex, but Calrod was different than all those guys. There was a quiet intensity to him that made me giddy in the strangest way.

Thankfully, Jasmine stopped bugging me, and we spent the rest of the afternoon setting up new items and helping the customers who came in buying several large pieces of furniture. The new ghostly arrivals mostly kept to themselves. I only had to save two vases and one trinket from being knocked off a table after the man in the top hat got irritated at some woman who knocked his painting off the wall. Jasmine never noticed a thing, too busy cataloging more items behind the front counter.

At closing time, Dagon headed out once Arkon showed up to take Jasmine home. She was talking about Morgan being here in the morning to open with me, but her words cut off on a sharp hiss. She went rigid, and Arkon was at her side in a second. She clutched his hand while he rubbed the small of her back, whispering to her until the episode passed. I stood by, wringing my hands, and hating there was nothing I could do for my friend. The panic attack ended, and Jasmine sagged into Arkon.

"I'm good," she mumbled. The look on my face must've been worse than I thought because she came to me and hugged me. "I promise, nothing is wrong with me more than normal."

I hugged her back, glancing at Arkon behind her. His lips were set in a thin line, and there were more furrows than usual to his creased brow. He was worried, and it wasn't simply because of the panic attack. His amber eyes flicked to me, and for a moment, I thought his face shifted, and his eyes glowed, just as I'd seen it do before. I flinched, but Jasmine was letting me go.

"I'll be in tomorrow afternoon," she said.

"How about you take a day off?" I suggested, and Arkon nodded.

"I'll be fine. And you," she said, whirling around on Arkon and pointing her finger at him, "stop it. I can still work, so I'm going to work."

"Cara and Morgan are more than willing to take over until you have the baby."

"It's true," I said, agreeing with Arkon. "How about you think on it?"

Jasmine crossed her arms, and I inwardly cursed at the look she gave me. "I'll consider it if you do the thing we talked about."

"That's playing dirty."

She shrugged, picked up her tote off the counter, and waddled for the door. "That's the deal, take it or leave it, woman. I'll see you tomorrow!" She waved over her shoulder, Arkon at her side, asking what deal we were talking about.

I watched them go, unable not to smile. Arkon had pulled Jasmine into his arms the moment they were outside and kissed her sweetly. Then he crouched, kissing her belly, too. Man, he never did seem like the cuddly, tender type, but there he was, being all of that and more.

I went around the shop, asking the spirits to please behave. They smiled at me, and the old record player kicked on. I watched them dance their way through the shop and let them be. I locked up the back door, turned off lights, and finally made my way out the front. Ensuring that door was locked up tight, I climbed into my hatchback and set off toward town. I hadn't gone to the grocery store yet and didn't really feel like doing it tonight. Figuring take-out four times a week wasn't that terrible, I swung by the quaint, family-run restaurant to pick something up. I parked along the curb and climbed out, digging through my purse for my wallet while I walked. The toe of my sneaker caught on the sidewalk, and I cursed, falling forward.

A hand snatched my elbow at the last second and swung me around. I found myself pressed against a hot and substantial chest. The hand on my elbow was also warm. It might be June, but suddenly, everything else felt cold except for where that hand held me.

I tilted my head back and was instantly captured by the blue eyes looking down at me. "Calrod."

"Maybe you should watch where you're walking," he said, his voice rumbling through his chest and a smile tugging at his lips.

"Probably a good idea," I agreed. His hand was still on my arm, and neither of us had backed away yet. His eyes narrowed slightly, slipping from my face and lower. He breathed out heavily through his nose, and the same warmth at his hand surrounded me. Unlike the humid heat of summer in Missouri, though, this heat somehow reached inside and set me on fire with a surge of want that left my thoughts fuzzy. "I uh, I was just grabbing some food," I managed to mumble.

"Food is good," he agreed quietly.

"Can be." Focus. I needed to focus. "I wanted to ask you something."

"What's that?"

Deciding Jasmine was right and there was no point in not asking, I licked my lips and blurted, "Would you want to try and come over to fix that damn sink this week?" I cringed. Damn it. I just had to chicken out at the last second. Hanging my head, I moved back, and his hand fell from my arm. Without the physical contact, goosebumps broke out on my arms, and I hugged myself, wishing I still had that heat.

Calrod's eyes brightened, then the sadness I was

so used to seeing returned. "I'll have to let you know if I have time. Been busier than usual with some larger projects."

"Oh yeah, course." I inwardly kicked myself. *Great, you lost your chance. Now he's avoiding you. Way to go, genius.*

"If anything changes, I'll let you know." He took another step back. "Enjoy your dinner."

Calrod walked down the street, a rigid set to his shoulders. Throwing my head back with a curse, I gave up on eating, climbed back into my car, and headed home.

"What's wrong with you?" I tossed my tote on the kitchen table along with my keys. "Can you fix my sink? God, could you sound any more like an idiot." Wrenching open the fridge, I snagged a beer, popped it open, and drank half of it down.

I ranted all the way through the house and out to the garage. My car had never been parked in here. I'd taken the space and turned it into a studio instead. On nice days, I opened the garage door and enjoyed the scenery around my cottage. Watching storms roll in while I worked the clay was a magical experience I'd never get tired of. A distant rumbling of thunder reached me, and I smiled, checking the radar on my phone. I hadn't expected a storm tonight, but the timing was perfect. Setting my beer down, I opened the garage, pulled on my heavy, green apron with its pockets holding my metal shaping tools, and set up the pottery wheel.

The kiln took up the corner near the door. A worktable occupied the wall to the right, and metal shelves lined the rest of the available wall space, most of them holding supplies. The rest were occupied with the pieces I'd made over the years. Vases mostly, a few small statuettes and figurines of various trees and flowers, wall hangings, and random things I threw together when I was in the mood to create. Crafting with clay had become my emotional outlet over the years. The second I sat down at the wheel, the rest of the world disappeared. Tonight, my mind was a mess, thanks to Calrod and me being too much of a coward to simply ask the man out when I'd had the chance. Hell, I should've done it months ago.

I slapped clay down on the wheel, and the first streak of lightning lit up the sky. Raindrops pattered the driveway not long after. My hands worked the clay while the wheel spun and the storm moved in. I shut my eyes, letting the noise carry me away, or I did until a cold touch brushed across my cheek.

"What? I'm fine."

The pale-faced figure that was only half visible shook her head, sending a cascade of pearly white hair tumbling over her shoulders.

"Don't give me that. You don't know what it's like dating now."

She rolled her eyes, planting her hands on her hips. Her legs were a wisp of mist, but the rest of her was detailed enough for me to see. Having a ghost in my cottage hadn't surprised me. I'd grown up being fascinated with the paranormal for more than one reason. When I was a kid, I thought I was just seeing things. Imaginary friends and whatnot. Then one day, I saw one of my classmates walking around town. Only he'd died in a car accident three years before. I never told anyone about what I could do. I'd avoid that awkward conversation with everyone for the rest of my life if possible. I was doing fine keeping my secret.

Seeing ghosts wasn't as terrifying as so many people made it out to be. The dead were undoubtedly around, but most of the time, they left the living alone. Jasmine's shop went through phases of having none to having over twenty, depending on what was in the shop.

Beth, the ghost who resided in my home, had been dead for almost a century. She'd been a wife and a mother but had tragically died when a man broke into their home. She'd protected her children but lost her life. The first time I saw her, she'd been so sad. Over the years, I managed to track down what had become of her family and how her line was very much alive. After that, she'd become highly interested in my life. I had parents, but they were retired and living on the east coast. Beth was like a second mom to me now. Not that I could tell anyone about her. They'd all think I was nuts.

Beth pressed her hand to my cheek again.

"I want to ask him out, but what if he's like Greg was?" I whispered, hating to bring up my cheating asshole of an ex.

She shrugged, the movement slow as if she were in water.

"Yeah, I know. Always a chance he could be and always a chance he's just what I'm looking for."

I did feel different around Calrod. Would asking him out really be the end of the world if he said no? Or if it didn't work out like I hoped? Absently, I returned to the clay, seeing Beth hovering around the garage out of the corner of my eye. She enjoyed watching me work. Not sure I was feeling up to making anything tonight, I eventually turned off the wheel.

Heavy footfalls sounded outside the garage, and I stilled. "Hello?"

I searched my apron for my phone, but I'd left it in the house. Shit. I stepped back, reaching for the button to close the garage. The footsteps came again, and I pressed the button. Lightning lit up the night, and my heart stuttered at the hulking monster standing on the driveway. It lunged forward, and the garage door went right back up. The overhead lights lit up a set of horns poking out of slicked back, red hair. Horns. The thing had horns. Long black claws extended from the hand it raised, pointing right at me. He opened his mouth, and red-stained fangs elongated while I watched. He wore a long black trench coat dripping from the rain.

"You're coming with me, witch," he said, his voice deep and rough.

My mind shouted at me to move, but my feet were rooted to the floor. Did he call me a witch? The word for what he had to be raced through my mind, but it couldn't be real. Shit, who was I kidding? I saw spirits daily. My mind yelled at me this beast was a demon. He came closer and closer, his laugh slamming into me like a punch to the gut. Then Beth appeared in front of him, waving her arms. Her trick sucked the warmth from the air. The demon snarled, and I rushed into the house, slamming and locking the door behind me. Furious yelling followed me, and I darted to the bedroom and my closet.

Gun. I had to get the shotgun.

I fumbled for the box of shells and was in the process of loading it but froze. The garage door crashed open, crashing into the kitchen wall. Clutching the shotgun, I pressed myself further into the closet and realized I didn't have to worry about Calrod anymore.

I was probably about to die.

3

Calrod

The nail split the wood plank in two, and I snarled, chucking it across the workshop.

"Just stop thinking about her," I ordered myself, snagging another piece of wood. "There's too much at risk. Carridan's coming, and if Cara gets too close, she'll get hurt, or worse. Think about something else. Anything else."

I was supposed to be building a set of bookshelves for the baby's nursery. Instead, all I'd done was create a mess in the shop at my house. For the last two weeks, I'd done a decent job of keeping my distance from Cara. The only times I saw her were at the store when it was my turn to watch over Jasmine. Somehow, I'd avoided being alone with her those days.

Then tonight, I had to run right into her. I was transported back to the night in the kitchen when I'd been so close to giving in. I almost did it there on the sidewalk, almost kissed her like I'd been dying to do for months. I set the nail in the board, brought the hammer down, and my cell went off. I missed the nail, smashing my finger instead. Snarling, I lobbed the hammer across the shop and snatched up my cell.

"What?"

"Cara's in trouble," Dagon said in a rush, and my inner fire roared in a fury for me. "We're too far away to reach her."

"Where?" I snapped, not bothering to ask questions. I snatched up my truck keys, darted out into the torrential downpour, and climbed into the old vehicle.

"Her house. There's a demon there. I can't see his face, but he's not there to be her friend."

"What else?"

"Nothing. It cut off right when he reached her. Calrod, be—"

Hanging up on him and cursing, I tossed my cell into the passenger seat and floored it away from my place and into the storm. It only took five minutes to reach Cara's cottage, but that was five minutes too many. Too many scenarios played out in my mind of what I'd find once I reached the house.

What if I was too late?

Snarling, I pressed the accelerator to the floorboard, willing myself to get there in time. I slammed on the brakes outside Cara's house and ran to the front door. Her scream came followed by several crashes. I kicked open the front door and charged in.

I recognized the demon immediately as one of Carridan's had Cara pinned to the wall, his hand around her neck. Her wide-eyed gaze shifted from him to me. The confusion flooding that look reminded me I hadn't bothered to put a glamour on before I rushed here. There was no point in doing it now, nor in trying to explain.

The demon wasn't about to be tucked out of sight while my fire bellowed with indignation of my mate being attacked.

The demon leered, clicking the claws of his free hand together. "Calrod, alive and well after all these years. I didn't expect to see you so early this evening.

Interesting your choice of company. Resorted to befriending witches now, is that it?"

His words caught me off guard, but there was no time to question them.

"Weston," I growled. He was one of Carridan's personal bloodhounds, a scout. If he was here, then Carridan wasn't going to be far behind. Not for long, at least. How did they know about Cara? Damn it, they must've been watching us longer than we thought. "Let her go."

Weston's hand flinched, and Cara flailed in his grasp. The house was a mess, with wrecked furniture scattered everywhere. A shotgun lay on the floor, broken into pieces. There were spent shells on the floor nearby. Blood covered Weston's right side, but it hadn't been nearly enough damage to bring him down.

"You're spoiling my fun. The plan was to torture her for a bit, then use her against you. You weren't part of the equation tonight." Weston's glowing green eyes narrowed, and he sighed. "Dagon and those obnoxious visions of his. Always ruining my well-laid plans."

My blood boiled and fire pooled in my hands.

"Going to resort to tricks, is that it? You think you can best me after all these years?"

"If I recall, I was always the one knocking you on your ass even without fire." I wanted to do more than catch the bastard on fire. Tearing his throat out with my fangs sounded like a great idea, too.

"Well, then, for old time's sake, why not put the flames away?"

Cara sputtered, struggling to breathe. The fire crept higher, coating my arms and burning dark blue. Hot enough to melt the flesh from Weston's body. My nostrils flared, and I tried to tell Cara without words that she was walking out of this house alive.

Weston looked over his shoulder at her, then back to me, chuckling in giddy delight.

"Oh, now that certainly changes everything. Not just a friend, then. My, my, Calrod. What would Vanessa think to know you'd moved on from her to this creature?"

I itched to charge across the room, but Weston was a sick bastard on par with the demon who'd tried to kill Jasmine. One wrong move and he'd snap Cara's neck. I'd lose her before I ever had a chance to see if she was to me who I believed her to be all these months.

Cara fumbled with the pockets of the apron she had on. I wasn't sure what she was trying to do, but

Weston kept his gaze locked onto me. Something silver flashed in the living room lights, then Weston snarled. He released Cara, and she crawled away, hacking and clutching her throat. Jutting out of Weston's arm was a metal rod of some kind. I didn't stop to figure out what it was.

I took my chance. I rushed forward while he yanked the tool free and tossed it aside. I slammed him into the wall, hand raised, ready to kill him. He ducked at the last second, and my fist went through the sheetrock.

Weston nailed me in the gut with his fist. I grunted but followed the hit with a head butt to his face. He cursed, swiping madly at me with a knife pulled from a sheath at his hip. I jumped back, avoiding a slash to my chest. I grabbed hold of his wrist and twisted his arm up and under. He raked the claws of his other hand down my side.

I wrenched his arm harder, and a satisfying crack filled the air. Letting his arm fall, I reached for his head next. He cursed, but it was too late. Viciously, I twisted, and his neck snapped. His limp body crashed to the floor. For good measure, I set him alight until there was nothing left but bones crackling away on the living room floor.

Hurrying around the corpse, I went to Cara. She had her back pressed to the wall, holding her throat and watching the flames consume Weston's body.

I hesitated, unsure if she'd realize who I was and that I wasn't a threat. "Cara?"

She was still coughing harshly, then looked at me. Where I expected to see fear, instead, there was anger, then she was scrambling off the floor. "Two," she rasped.

"What?"

"Two—Calrod!"

Claws buried into my shoulders, throwing me across the room.

Cara shouted. I pushed off the floor, flames burning even darker blue in my hands at the sight of a second demon going for Cara. I didn't recognize his face. Not that it mattered. He hauled her off the floor, but she dug her thumbs into his eyes until he released her. He staggered, raising his arm and back-handing her. She flew across the room, hitting the couch and tipping it over.

Enraged, I roared and charged right into the bastard. My fists collided with his face. We fought to tear each other apart. Blood spurted from slash wounds and punctures, but neither of us went down.

He was my height with a bit more heft to his shoulders. I caught a fist to the nose, then another to the kidney. I aimed a burning hand at his chest, but the flames bounced off as if they'd hit a wall. He smirked, and the red amulet hanging around his neck lit up.

Furious, I threw myself forward, aiming for the gold chain. His knee pounded into my gut, and his fist came up under my jaw. I backed off, motioning him to keep coming. He did, attacking until his eyes bulged, and he moved far faster than before.

That was all I needed. For him to make a mistake. Just one mistake.

Another punch to the sternum sent me stumbling into the front door. I winced, pain shooting down my spine. But the demon was getting tired. I waited, luring him in closer. A scream was the only warning I had, then Cara leaped onto his back, stabbing at his neck with whatever she had in her hand. He howled, whipping around to yank her off. When that failed, he backed into the doorframe by the kitchen. She hit her head and fell to the floor, not moving.

"No!" Flames coated my hands, and I forgot about my plan to let the demon make a mistake.

Cara hadn't gotten up yet. I couldn't even tell if she was breathing.

The demon spun around.

I gave him a wicked grin. During Cara's attack, the chain to his amulet had snapped.

"Where's your protection now, asshole?"

He growled, but I was faster. Bright blue flames shot from my hands, wrapping around his body. His growl turned into a scream as the fire ate at his skin, then the muscles beneath. The fire pulsed hotter, roaring as if it were alive. In all my years, I'd never created such intense flames before. If I had any doubts about what I felt for Cara, I didn't any longer. My fire was more than willing to admit what she meant to me, even if the rest of me continued to hesitate.

When only charred bones remained, I pulled the fire back into my hands. The demon's skeleton tumbled to the floor, his skull rolling to my feet. I crushed it under my boot, grinding it to dust. Burning them also meant there was nothing left on their persons to search and give us answers.

Too late to worry about that now.

Kneeling at Cara's side, I let out a breath of relief to see her chest rising and falling. "Cara?" Gently, I shook her shoulder and held her bruised cheek in my palm. "Cara? Let me see your eyes, woman." Gingerly, I shifted my hand through her hair, feeling the back of her head. There was a bump, but thankfully, no blood. She was damned lucky.

Her brow furrowed and she groaned. "Ow."

I smiled in relief, then froze. I still looked like a demon, like the monsters who attacked her. I was about to put my glamour back in place, but her eyes opened, and she looked right at me. I held my breath, too worried about her reaction to move.

"Calrod?"

"Yeah, there's uh, there's a few things we should probably talk about."

"Just a few?" She winced, scrunching her eyes shut. When she opened them again, there was still no fear in them.

I didn't smell any on her either. How was she not terrified?

"Like how you're not human?" she added quietly, glancing up at my horns.

"That'd be one of them."

Slowly, she sat up. I helped her, then shifted away to give her space. She held her head, cursing under her breath. Blood speckled her hands and her clothes. Unsure if any of it was hers had my palms growing hot and my fire ready to burst free. I clenched my fists on my thighs, hoping she didn't notice the black smoke slipping from between my fingers. The silence became deafening while she glanced from me to the two burned demons behind me, then to my smoking hands. Her blank face made it impossible for me to figure out what she was thinking.

Then she opened her mouth, and the questions tumbled out so fast, there was no time to attempt to answer any of them. I held up my hand, and she clamped her mouth shut mid-sentence. Her eyes widened, and I grunted, annoyed, at the blue flame dancing in the center of my palm. Quickly, I smothered it but doubted it'd be the last errant flame to appear tonight.

"That was real," she whispered. "You can what, control fire? Shit, Calrod, what is all of this? Why were they even here? What are they? What are you?"

"Demon," I said, and she pressed her back into the wall. "I'm a demon, and so are—*were*—they."

Her eyes danced from my face, taking in my horns again, then down to my hands and my black claws. Her eyes lit up, and she barked a laugh. "I knew there was something weird about you guys."

I blinked, sure I'd heard her wrong. "What did you say?"

"You and your brothers? None of you act normal. I've spotted blue fire shimmering in your eyes a few times. Now I know why. Then there's the growling, which all of you suck at hiding, and I was sure the other day I saw Arkon looking different when I came into the shop. Today, too. Happens when he gets really annoyed with Jasmine. Explains a lot, actually," she mused, her lips curling into a smile.

"Just wait a second," I said, trying to catch up with what she was saying. "You knew?"

"Not that you were demons, but that you obviously weren't ordinary."

"This doesn't freak you out?" I asked, motioning to myself and the dead demons behind me.

"Oh, I never said that," she replied. "I'm pretty sure I'm losing my mind right now. Yep, I've finally lost it. First, it was seeing dead people and now demons. Life can't get any stranger, right? Man, I really liked that rug."

"Forget about the damn rug." I reached for her but pulled back at the last second. The rest of what she said hit me, and I frowned. "You see dead people?"

"Huh?" She was looking past me. "Hang on. Yeah, Beth, I got it."

"Beth?" I turned around, but we were alone.

"She lives here. Kinda looks out for me." Cara was still looking across the room, but there was nothing there as far as I could see or sense. "I'm okay. I know you couldn't do more. Looks like I have a guardian demon anyway." She laughed, slumping against the wall. "Damn, my head hurts. There's a lot happening right now. I could use a drink or five."

Using the wall, she hauled herself up, wobbling on her feet. I steadied her, and she didn't even flinch at my touch.

"You're always so warm," she whispered. "Is that because you're a demon or because of the fire?"

"Both," I replied slowly, waiting for her to start screaming at me to get out.

"You look about as confused as I feel." She patted my shoulder and made her way to the kitchen. "Nice that your flames didn't burn down the whole house." She pulled two beers out of the fridge, set them on the table, and yanked open the freezer next. She grabbed a bag of frozen corn and pressed it to the right side of her face. "That's going to leave a mark tomorrow."

I leaned against the doorframe, watching her.

She winced as she adjusted the bag and I couldn't stand it any longer. I crossed the room in three strides and eased the bag of corn off her face to examine the marks left behind by the fight. Nothing was broken, but that was a small comfort. She'd attacked both demons seemingly without a care for her safety. The urge to lecture her had the words on my tongue, but I turned them into a grunt at the last second. She wasn't *with* me. I had no right to call her out for throwing herself onto a demon's back with, hell, I didn't even know what she used to attack him.

My thumb brushed over her neck, knowing it'd be black and blue in the morning. I shifted my hand higher, lightly tracing the red mark on her jaw that would be one hell of a bruise, too.

She sighed, her eyes closing while she rested against the counter.

"That feels nice," she whispered.

I moved her messed-up hair out of the way, searching her face for more injuries. I checked her hands next. Aside from some busted knuckles, she'd made it out unscathed. When I tried to let go, her hand squeezed mine.

"Don't. Not yet. If you let go, I might end up on the floor."

Pulled to her by an invisible force, I shifted closer until our bodies barely brushed against one another. She opened her eyes, tilting her head back to look up at me.

"How do you make yourself look different?"

"Glamour spell," I said. I rolled my shoulders, and the spell fell into place.

She blinked, shaking her head. "You look weird."

"Hence the glamour," I said, but she shook her head again. "The glamour looks weird?"

She shrugged. "Your eyes, your voice? The way you move? They never matched the way you looked. I thought I was being odd, but now it makes sense. Can you make it go away?"

The spell shattered, and I stood before her as the demon I was.

She smiled, reaching a tentative hand toward my face. I'd imagined this moment so many times. Never did I expect to feel as I did with her hand pressing to my cheek. Not my glamoured face, but my real one. My muscles tensed, then relaxed while her fingers traced my jawline and higher to my cheekbone. Her other hand joined the first, following the lines of my face and into my hair. She had to stand on her toes to reach the horns atop my head. At first contact, a rush of desire left me burning. My hands fumbled for the edge of the counter behind her, clutching it fast in my fists and burying my claws into the butcher block top.

"Sorry," she whispered, drawing back. "Does that hurt?"

"Not even close," I growled.

Her eyes darkened. She bit her lip, and I forgot we'd just been in a fight with demons in her living room. I forgot that she was just now seeing me for who I truly was. All that mattered was claiming the woman I'd wanted since the first time I saw her.

I lowered my head the same time she rose even higher on her toes. Our mouths met, and my heart thundered away in my chest. Her lips were soft and demanding while her hands grabbed hold of my horns. I snagged her hips, taking control and plunging my tongue into her mouth. Hers was there to greet me, stoking the fire that already burned so hot inside my soul.

I lifted her onto the counter, and she dragged me into her arms. I pressed my hands to the flat of her back, desperate to feel more skin. The wall I'd put up to stop myself from getting close to her blew up in my face. I shouldn't be doing this, but nothing I told myself made me stop.

Cara dug her heels into my ass. My hands slipped to her thighs, massaging them through the denim, then pulling her to me. I knew the second she felt my swollen shaft in my jeans. She shifted her hips, and I ground against her in kind. How bad would it really be to give in?

Her fingers dug into my shoulders, and I growled at the sharp stab of pain. "Shit, sorry." She broke the kiss, staring worriedly at the puncture wounds. "I need to take care of those."

"They're fine."

She didn't seem so sure but started to come back to kiss me again. I slipped from her arms, set her hands on her lap, and backed to the other side of the room.

"Calrod?"

Her lips were red from our kiss, and her flushed face almost had me right back in her arms.

"We need to talk about a few things," I said. "Or everything."

"Yeah, talking. Right. That's probably a good idea."

Her disappointed look had me shuffling my feet. Why had I given in and kissed her? It shouldn't have happened, but too damn late now. I wasn't sure what else to say or where to even start.

The house phone rang.

Cara jumped. She reached across the counter for the cordless.

"Hello? Dagon, just slow down," she said in a

rush. "He's right here." She held it out for me, and I took it.

"Yeah?"

"You weren't answering your damn phone," Dagon shouted. "What happened?"

"A lot," I replied, holding Cara's gaze. "I think we need to have a family meeting, and someone needs to call Cyrene." I whispered to Cara if she was okay with everyone coming over, and she laughed, slipping off the counter.

"Why the hell not? Let's make it a party."

I scowled at her reply but told Dagon to have everyone meet here. He hung up, and I set the phone on the counter. Cara was in the living room, hands on her hips, muttering about how you were supposed to clean up burnt demon corpses. This night could've gone worse, but as it was, I had no idea what she was really thinking about all of this. What I wanted to do was drag her right back into my arms and kiss her, but that was out of the question until we talked. We had to talk.

After that, I had no idea what would happen. It was too late to stop Cara from getting pulled into this shit storm. If Carridan's demons came after her once, they'd do it again, all to get to me, or maybe not. Weston had called her a witch. After learning she could see dead people, I supposed that was true. I knew I should've tried harder to stay away.

Cara might not betray me as someone else had, but a relationship with her was going to end the same way. Heartache. I wasn't sure I could survive it a second time, especially if it ended with her getting killed because of me.

4

———

Cara

"Will you stop looking at me like that?"

I arched a brow and I crossed my arms at Jasmine. "How do you want me to look at you?"

"Not like that."

"You could've told me all of this months ago," I argued.

"Told you what exactly? That my boyfriend is a demon, and by the way, so are his brothers. Oh, and I might be a witch, and we're also friends with a witch, and hey, one more thing, they've all been on the run for years because some crazy demon prince is trying to kill them?" she ranted, sucking in a breath at the end of it. "Yeah, that would've been a great conversation. Besides, you're one to talk."

"Me? What did I lie to you about?"

"Gee, I don't know, maybe the fact that you freaking see dead people."

A loud whistle cut through the air, and we turned to glower at Dagon, his fingers still held to his lips.

"Damn, how about we all just take it down a notch? You're going to put yourself into early labor," he muttered, pointing to Jasmine's stomach, "and you're going to give yourself a coronary."

"I'm mad at you, too," I muttered but sighed. "I'm sorry, Jas. I just can't believe you didn't trust me enough to tell me the truth."

"Can you blame me?"

I wanted to say yes, but looking around my living room now, that'd be a lie. After Dagon called the house to check on Calrod and me, it didn't take long for them all to show up. Dagon and Morgan had gotten here first since they'd already been on their way over, terrified we were both dead. Arkon and Jasmine showed up a few minutes after. At the sight of the two charred corpses in my living room, Arkon had unleashed a torrent of words I didn't understand at Calrod, who answered in the same rough, guttural language. Jasmine had hugged me, asking me if I was alright. I'd had no good way to respond and still wasn't sure.

Just like Calrod, Arkon and Dagon had used glamour spells to hide their appearances. I'd told them to drop them. There was no point hiding anymore. Seeing them in their true forms hadn't been much of a shock after nearly being killed by two demons and seeing Calrod rush in with his demon in full view. I'd gotten the rundown on the brothers' abilities, as well as what Morgan could do. I'd had one drink already, but a few more were starting to sound like a great idea. So many secrets.

I glanced at Calrod. He stood across the room, his eyes pointedly looking at the floor. Since everyone else had arrived, he'd kept his distance from me. It was irritating, though I wasn't entirely sure why. Did he think I was scared of him? He shouldn't, especially after what we did in the kitchen. In those few seconds, I'd forgotten about the charred corpses in my living room. I'd been more than ready to give in to the desire that had been coursing through me since the first time I met him. And god, his skin was so warm, I honestly never thought someone could physically feel like that.

But there was more to it. I wanted him back beside me, needed him there, but Jasmine was talking again.

"You're sure these were Carridan's demons?" she asked Calrod.

"Yeah, though they didn't exactly give me a chance to sit down and chat," Calrod snapped.

Arkon growled.

Calrod swiped a hand down his face. "Sorry, it's just, they shouldn't have come here."

"Why did they?" I asked.

Calrod's eyes shimmered with blue fire, flicking to me for a split second then away again. "To get to me."

The demon who'd nearly strangled me to death had said some odd things. Like my being a witch, and something about Calrod moving on from Vanessa to me? Was she an ex of his? I puffed out my cheeks, not sure blurting out that we had no relationship to talk of was entirely relevant right then. There could be, but with how he was acting now, I wasn't sure he could push past whatever held him back. Then there was the kiss. Had I started that, or had he? Did it even matter? Head spinning, I sank to the couch, holding my throbbing skull between my hands.

"You're handling this pretty well," Jasmine assured me, rubbing my back.

"Yeah? I feel like I'm losing it."

"Trust me, you could be taking it a lot worse," Jasmine said. "Just keep breathing, and you'll be fine. You should be celebrating after surviving your first fight with some demons."

"Yeah. Our encounters didn't end so well," Morgan added. "Jasmine was technically dead, and I have some gnarly scars now."

Arkon and Dagon growled, but it was Calrod's snarl that dominated the room, bouncing off the living room walls. My head shot up at the burning heat pressing into my back. He wasn't there, but it felt like it all the same. Arkon muttered something to him, but it was in that language again. Calrod's lip twitched, and he stormed out of the living room and into the kitchen. His brothers exchanged a glance then followed, saying they'd be right back.

"Is there something else I'm missing?" I asked. "Calrod looks ready to go hunt down more of these assholes and set them on fire."

"That can happen," Morgan chimed in, then winced, rubbing her temples. "Damn. I wish Dagon would take him outside, though. His anger is sharp tonight. And his fear is making me sick."

"Fear? Fear of what? You should've seen him," I exclaimed, pointing to the remains. "I've never seen someone fight—well, ever—but the way he moved was like a man possessed. Or a demon. Can demons be possessed? Is that a thing?"

Jasmine's mouth opened and closed a couple of times, then she laughed. "No wonder Calrod's out of sorts with you right now."

"What are you talking about?"

"During the fight, I'm going to assume you didn't just let him handle the situation," Jasmine elaborated.

"Why would I do that? They came after me in my own damn house. He needed help."

Morgan and Jasmine exchanged a long look.

"So you put yourself in harm's way," Morgan said, nodding slowly. "That explains the fear he's feeling."

"Fear of what?"

"Losing you," she replied. "Why do you think Dagon called Calrod to come over and save you tonight? And he came without question to protect you. It's not just because he's a nice guy, Cara. It's never that simple with demons."

My thoughts took a second to catch up to what she was saying. When they did, my cheeks burned, and I flew off the couch, pacing around the living room. I nearly stepped on the burned-up corpses twice and forced myself to come to a stop by the front door.

"Did something else happen before we got here?" Jasmine pushed.

I shoved my hands in my apron pockets. "Nothing."

"Cara."

I mulled over my chances of getting out of this conversation easily and gave in. It was better not to argue with the temperamental pregnant woman. "We might've kissed, but it wasn't just a kiss. I mean, it was, but it was like a hot, fiery, in-your-face kiss. Which I guess all kisses are like that, but yeah. It was great, and I like him, alright? Are you trying to say he likes me like you know really likes me? Wow, I sound like a pathetic teenager."

"A little bit," Jasmine said, laughing, "but yeah, he likes you."

"And when a demon likes someone like *that,* things can get touchy for them in certain respects."

My brow shot up, waiting for Morgan to elaborate. When she didn't, I motioned at her to get on with it. She hesitated, and I was ready to start throwing things at her. A gust of wind whipped through the living room, bringing with it a burst of green leaves that fell to the floor.

"She means Calrod has found his mate."

I jumped at the voice coming from behind me. I whirled around, coming face to face with a smiling woman. Her violet hair was dragged back in several intricate braids interwoven with green ribbons and glistening silver beads. Behind her stood a man, his skin a gorgeous shade of green and covered in tattoos that shifted as if alive.

"Uh, hi," I mumbled. "Who are you?" I blurted, then shook my head. "Wait, back up. You said mate. As in what, soul mates? I'm Calrod's mate?" A part of me said that was shit of fairy tales, but I did have a house currently filled with demons and a ghost—and witches, apparently. At this point, it was easier to accept the latest bombshell than argue with it. "How long has he known this?"

The woman's grin widened, her violet eyes sparkling. "I like this one."

"Cara, this is Cyrene," Morgan said, motioning to the violet-haired woman. "That's Rik."

"You're not demons."

"No, dear, I'm a witch, and Rik is a fae."

I blinked. "Okay, I guess I shouldn't be surprised."

"Not since you apparently talk to dead people," Jasmine muttered from the couch.

"Are you ever going to let that go?" I threw at her over my shoulder.

"You tell me. Wait," she said, her eyes widening, "are there ghosts in the shop right now?"

"Just a few, but they're harmless. And I only have one living with me. Beth. She's pretty nice. Looks out for me. She faded out after everyone showed up." I threw my hands upward, turning back to Cyrene. "Can we get back to the whole mate thing? No one's giving me straight answers."

Cyrene lay her hands on my shoulders. Immediately a sense of calm washed over me. "It means if you give yourself to him, and he, in turn, does the same, he'll never let you go. He'll be yours, and you'll be his for all time. Demons don't let go of what's theirs, not easily. Well, not ever, actually. And they guard it with a fierce passion."

When I glanced their way, Jasmine and Morgan were nodding and smiling. Some of Calrod's behavior tonight made sense now. What didn't was why he kept trying to push me away if I was his mate or whatever. We'd kissed in the kitchen, but he'd barely looked at me since. Did he not want to be mated to me? Was that a thing? Even more curious was why I wasn't freaking out over the fact that apparently, I had a mate. I kept expecting the ridiculousness of that sentence to hit me, but it never did. It felt right in the strangest way. Calrod had intrigued me from day one. The idea that we bumped into each other for a reason was comforting. Or I was merely losing what sanity I had. My mind was in shambles, and the mad urge to giggle rose up. I started to let it out, then stopped, clapping a hand over my mouth.

"You're in good company," Jasmine assured me. "Taking in all of this isn't easy."

"But you've got us," Morgan promised. "And you've got Calrod."

"Do I?" I asked, hating the disappointment that darkened my tone.

Jasmine gave me a worried frown but heavy steps headed toward the living room. I didn't have to look up to know Calrod stood there, his brothers beside him. The weight of his presence was more than enough to tell me he was here, and he was far from alright.

"Cyrene," Calrod said, and I finally lifted my eyes from the floor. His gaze flicked to me, his jaw working like he was struggling not to say more.

"Calrod. It would appear you've been keeping things from me," Cyrene replied.

His eyes narrowed, and he growled. "We have more important concerns."

"I'm afraid I have to disagree with you. These things can't be put on hold or avoided. I don't understand how all three of you thought they could be. It only makes things harder on everyone involved."

I had no idea what she was talking about. The three brothers appeared to, however, and glowered until Cyrene's brow arched.

Arkon and Dagon slipped away from Calrod and went to Jasmine and Morgan.

"I can't do this, not now," Calrod argued.

"Why?" she asked.

Calrod snarled, motioning to the dead demons in my living room. "Why do you think? If Carridan's scouts are already in Oak Hollow, how long do you think until he shows up himself? I knew I should've kept my distance and now look what's happened."

"This is about me, isn't it," I said, and Calrod's eyes flared with blue flames. "Take that as a yes."

"We need a plan for when Carridan arrives," Calrod said, his voice growing rougher by the second. "Can we do that? Please?"

Cyrene looked ready to march across the room and smack him, but she gave in. "Very well. It would appear the warding I've established around Oak Hollow is not as strong as I'd hoped. I'll have to come up with something more potent. To do so, I may need help. Arkon, Morgan, you two are the most adept at magic. I'll need your assistance. And I'll contact a few other witches, see who's available. Jasmine, until you've had the baby, I'm afraid your magic is of no use to me yet."

"What magic?" Jasmine muttered. "Still not sure I believe you."

Cyrene winked. "All in good time. Think of your magic as preoccupied right now."

"And before that?" Jasmine asked.

"It's complicated," Cyrene said simply.

"You think they know about us, too, or just got lucky with seeing Cara and Calrod?" Morgan asked.

"I think it's safe to assume Arkon and Dagon are being watched as closely as Calrod. Though it'd be nice to know how they're seeing you all. I suppose they could have a witch or two working with them," Cyrene said. "Either way, I'd prefer us not to be caught off guard again."

"You're sure the warding around the town will be strong enough to keep them out this time?" Arkon had hold of Jasmine's hand. She was leaning into his side, trying to comfort him, but it didn't seem to be working.

"He's a prince of the Underworld," Cyrene said quietly. "The magic we're going to have to use will, unfortunately, take time if we're going to have a hope of keeping him away. And that's only if he's not coming to Oak Hollow bearing magic of his own. Soul Piercer isn't the only ancient weapon floating around the human world."

"You're worried," Morgan whispered, and Cyrene's violet eyes narrowed. "Not just about us."

"Something else you've been keeping from us?" Calrod demanded.

"Don't take that tone with me," Cyrene snapped, and the air crackled while the leaves she'd brought with her kicked up and swirled around her feet. "You might be a prince of the Underworld, but I'm not simply a witch who lives in the woods."

I wasn't the only one who straightened at her words.

Jasmine gave Arkon a confused glance. Dagon and Morgan seemed unsure what Cyrene might mean. Calrod bristled, his lip twitching. From their reactions, there were more secrets that even they didn't know. Inwardly I sighed. All secrets ever did was hurt everyone in the end. But I didn't know

Cyrene, and I wasn't about to call out the witch who could probably squash me out of existence with a word.

"Now, I suggest we come up with a plan on how to proceed," Cyrene said firmly.

The tense conversation that followed turned into one about magic. I tried to follow it but gave up after ten minutes. I shifted my attention to Calrod's stiff form instead. He'd remained by the kitchen, his arms crossed so tightly across his chest, he had to be cramping by now. Each time he spoke, his voice was little more than a growl, and the glowing to his eyes only turned darker with each scenario they laid out for if and when this Prince Carridan showed up.

Eventually, the brothers and Cyrene came up with a plan. Setting up magical booby traps around town to capture the intruders was their best option since they'd be outnumbered. No one had to say what would happen then. The murderous intent had been plain enough in the brothers' eyes. Nor did anyone have to say there was a chance none of these preparations would work. They were grasping at straws, and I wondered how powerful this Carridan guy really was.

With a snap of Cyrene's fingers, the charred corpses of the demons vanished from sight. She clapped her hands, giving herself a satisfied nod. "Now then, if you'll excuse me, I have quite a bit of work ahead of me yet this night. Morgan, Arkon, I suggest you get some rest, too," Cyrene told them. "Cara, you and I will be speaking more, too, about this ability of yours and where it will lead you."

I nodded, not sure what to even say to that.

Calrod shifted forward, opening his mouth to speak, but she beat him to it.

"Don't insult her by asking me that question, Calrod. One way or another, she would've been pulled into this conflict. Be happy it was sooner. There's time at least for her to understand. For both of you to." She bade us all goodnight and waved her hand. The same gust of wind and leaves that brought Cyrene and Rik to my house erupted again. When the leaves fell, the two of them were gone.

"She always do that?" I asked.

"Always," Arkon muttered.

"You get used to it," Jasmine added. She yawned, stretching her arms over her head. "Damn, I'm exhausted. We should probably head out. Welcome to the party, Cara." She hugged me one more time, gave Calrod a look I didn't quite understand, and let Arkon guide her out the door.

Morgan smacked Dagon on the shoulder, not too

subtly tilting her head toward the exit. "Right, we should get going, too. Lots to plan and what not if we all want to survive," Dagon said with a bright smile. "Night!"

"Night," I said lamely, watching them go next. I waited for Calrod to follow his brothers. He didn't move from his place in the living room. After thirty seconds, I clasped my hands, rocking on my feet. "I'm sure you're beat, too. You heading home to get some sleep? Maybe you want to make sure those wounds you refused to let me look at aren't festering."

He pinned me to the spot with a sharp look. "You were just attacked by two demons in your own home because of me. Do you honestly think I'm leaving you alone?"

"Good point."

I blew out a breath, then smacked my lips shut. My stomach growled, and I realized I hadn't eaten anything since lunch. The kitchen clock said half past midnight, but I wasn't even close to tired. I wandered to the fridge and tugged it open, my gaze absently wandering over the shelves. Nothing looked good, and I tried the pantry next. My eyes landed on the jar of peanut butter. Figuring it was better than nothing, I twisted off the top, tossed it on the counter, and dug around in the drawer for a spoon. Digging out a heap of creamy butter, I hopped up on the kitchen counter and enjoyed my late-night snack. I was onto my third spoonful by the time I realized Calrod had joined me. With the spoon shoved in my mouth, I glanced up. His blue eyes were glowing, much as they had all night, but this look was far different.

This look was the same one he had while we kissed.

"You do this often?" he asked quietly.

"Don't judge me for my peanut butter habits. Could be worse. I could be drunk on my ass right now," I said, waving the spoon at the bottles of whiskey and tequila lining the shelf on the wall. "So, are we going to talk?"

"Not much else to talk about."

"Hmm, not true."

He grunted and slumped into one of the kitchen chairs.

"Tell me what Cyrene meant," I said, and Calrod frowned. "Right before she left, she told you something about you asking her a question. What was she talking about?"

"No idea."

"Uh-huh. And the other thing she said about

me getting dragged into this conflict one way or the other? I doubt she was referring to me seeing dead people. I've avoided witches and demons this long, so she had to be talking about something else."

"She's a witch," he said, tapping his black claws on the table. "She and others like her say all sorts of nonsense constantly. You shouldn't listen to it."

I set the peanut butter down, tossing my spoon into the sink with a loud clank. "I might be new to this whole demons and witches, and whatever exists in the world, but I'm not stupid. And I guess technically, I've known about magic and shit since I can talk to dead people. Point is," I went on while his face became a blank mask, "you and I need to have a conversation. An honest one."

His lips remained tightly shut, but the temperature in the room rose.

"Have you been pushing me away all these months because of the whole I'm your—"

"Don't say it," he cut me off, his hand flattening to the table.

"Why not?" The sensation of being rejected was like a punch to the gut. I slid off the counter, unsure of myself right then. Realizing I still had on my apron from earlier, I removed it, hanging it on the hook by the garage door. "Unless it's you don't want me to be—"

"Not what I said," he whispered quietly.

"No?"

The chair legs scraped across the floor, and I felt how close he was without lifting my head. "Saying it aloud is admitting what I've felt for you, toward you, is real, and I can't go through this right now. Look what's already happened to you because of me. I'm a demon, Cara."

"And I'm a freak who sees dead people. None of us are perfect."

"Do you even hear yourself right now?"

"I don't see the problem." Steadily, I held his gaze, noting the weight of sadness in those blue depths. That sadness had nothing to do with this Carridan guy. "What happened to you?"

"You heard the story," he said, but I shook my head.

"No, I'm not talking about your parents, or Carridan, or you guys being on the run all these years. You faced something else, and that's why you kept pushing me away. You had no idea Carridan would've found you, so you had no reason to not give in to what you're feeling." I reached for his hand, but he yanked it back. "When we kissed earlier, it wasn't just physical contact between two people. It was fierce and alive, and I've never felt like that with anyone. Why are you so afraid to feel it with me?"

"I told you," he murmured. "I'm keeping my distance for your sake."

"No, you're not, but if you want to keep lying to yourself and me, fine. Have at it." Exhaustion crashed into me, and I moved around him toward the door. "You can have the guest room. I'm going to bed."

His hand closed around my elbow, stopping me from leaving the kitchen. "I wanted to tell you the truth about me so many times," he said softly, "but I never thought you'd take it so well."

"What? You really expected me to go screaming for the hills?" I asked with a laugh.

His brow furrowed even more, and his hand slipped from my elbow until he was holding my hand. "I knew the second you crashed into me after falling off that damn ladder you were mine," he growled, and a bubble of heat started in my gut. "You can't possibly understand the gravity of what that means after one night."

"Try me." I turned, so I faced him fully. "You think you're the only one that had the same feeling?"

"You barely know me."

"Then talk to me," I insisted. "I'm right here, Calrod. Tell me the truth, tell me whatever you want, just talk to me instead of pushing me away. I'll admit I haven't exactly been the smoothest when it comes to asking you out either, but I'm willing to dive head-first into this mess right now. You really going to stand there and let me do it alone?"

The words were barely out of my mouth, then I was in his arms. His growl vibrated through my body while his mouth covered mine in a kiss that had me sure I had to be on fire. I clung to his arms, digging my nails into his biceps. He grunted, a primal sound that sent a shiver of anticipation down my spine. He backed me into the living room, deepening the kiss with each step we took. The couch bumped my legs, and he spun us around, sank onto the cushions, and dragged me down after him. His hands wandered under my shirt. The heat radiating from him flowed through me, and I sighed, melting even more. His arousal was more than evident between my legs, and I ground my hips into his. I'd never wanted anything more in my life than I wanted Calrod right then, naked and inside me. The worries I'd been carrying around about us not working out together vanished in a puff of smoke.

How could he not want to give in to what I knew he felt?

I tugged at his t-shirt and started to pull it over his head. He caught my hands, breaking away from me with a curse. He sat me on the couch and stormed to the far side of the room. A bluish haze surrounded him, and his eyes were the brightest I'd seen them yet.

"You should get some rest," he muttered.

"Fine." I stood up, lips tingling and body on fire. "I'm not sure what you're running from, but I'm not going anywhere. Not until I understand what this is between us. I'll be right here when you're ready."

"That's the problem," he whispered. "The closer you are to me, the more danger you're in. You're acting like this situation is easy, but it's not. I wish you were terrified. Maybe then you'd understand how serious this all is."

"I'm not taking any of this lightly."

"Sure as hell could've fooled me," he argued hotly.

"Sorry that I've learned to simply roll with what's thrown at me instead of cowering in a corner. If I'd done that, I never would've left my room again. I never would've kept going. I never said I wasn't scared, but I'm not about to suddenly throw my hands up and say, 'That's it guys, I quit.' I'm not some frail damsel in distress."

"I never said you were, but this isn't just about seeing spirits anymore. This is witches and magic and demons out for blood. You could've lost your life today. You get that, right?"

"I didn't because I have you."

"You're putting far too much faith in someone you don't know."

The guilt and sadness warred in his eyes and the lines etched on his face. I longed to go to him, but I sensed pushing him tonight would get me nowhere but more frustrated. I aimed for the hall leading to the bedrooms but paused. "Thanks, by the way."

"For what?"

"Keeping me alive. I'll see you in the morning." I didn't wait for a reply but headed to my room and shut the door.

I changed into a tank and sleep shorts, climbed into bed, and finally let the swell of emotions hit me. Hoping Calrod couldn't hear my mad quiet giggles followed by a few moments of crying, I curled up with one of my pillows, shut my eyes, and hoped for a dreamless night of sleep.

5

———

Calrod

Glaring at the ceiling in the guest bedroom, I finally understood why Arkon and Dagon vented to me so much about Morgan and Jasmine. Having a mate wasn't a stroll in the park, not even close. I hadn't been able to fall asleep, too busy replaying the moment Cara threw herself onto the demon's back. Watching her slammed into the doorframe and slumping to the floor again.

I sat up with a quiet growl, holding my head in my hands. A small part of me admired Cara for not running from the house, screaming. She'd stood her ground and fought back, but what if I hadn't gotten there in time? What if I'd fallen during that fight? She'd be dead.

Not counting on sleep tonight, I picked up my t-shirt from the floor, pulled it over my head, and padded quietly through the house to Cara's room. Easing the bedroom door open, I peered inside. She was snoring quietly, hugging a pillow to her chest while she slept. The moonlight played off her black hair sprawled over her shoulders and highlighted the curve of her cheek. The sight of her brought an unbidden smile to my face as it always did. My pulse raced a little quicker, and the fire that was a part of me flickered in my palms.

Kissing her had awakened a primal desire I'd buried deep. All I wanted was to do it again. Hold her close while I explored every last inch of her body. Giving in for those brief moments had me desperate to feel her lips against mine all over again. To bury myself deep inside her while we claimed each other. It wasn't hard to imagine what it'd be like. The quiet moans she'd made when we kissed echoed in my mind, setting my body off. Not being near her left me shaky. I was two steps into her room, ready to wake her with a soft kiss before my sanity returned with a jolt.

Everything Cyrene said was right. Putting off being with Cara was only going to make it harder on all of us. But even Cyrene didn't know the whole story. I'd told no one and was extremely careful not to let those thoughts surface whenever I was around her or Dagon or anyone else who could glean thoughts from my head.

It wasn't that I didn't want to admit I had a mate. It was the fact that I didn't deserve one. Being happy, having that kind of life wasn't a future I saw for myself.

Quietly, I pulled the door closed and walked through the house to the kitchen. Roughly, I rubbed my hands over my face, noting the scruff on my cheeks. I hadn't shaved in a few days, not that Cara seemed to mind. Merely thinking of her took me right back to how we'd been together in this room.

Flipping on the light, I figured I'd get a pot of coffee going and get back to fixing the sink. After seeing Cara make it enough times, I knew where the grounds were. With the coffee brewing, I was going to search for the few tools she had in her laundry room—

The light shut off in the kitchen.

Curious, I flipped the switch back on. "Cara?"

There was no answer, and the house was silent

around me. Shrugging, I returned to the laundry room, but the light shut off a second time. Worried the house was going to be attacked, I summoned fire to my hands. I crept forward, one slow step at a time. An icy touch brushed across the back of my neck, and I knew I wasn't alone. Damn. What did Cara say the ghost's name was?

"Beth?" I asked, and the light flipped back on. "I'll take that as a yes."

I'd never spoken to spirits. Being a demon meant I could sort of sense when they were near if they wanted to make themselves known, but none of them ever reached out to me. I never had a reason to bother them. The cold touch came at my neck again. I turned, catching a mist hanging in the air.

"If you're worried about Cara, she's alright."

The chair scooted out from the table, and the painting on the wall rattled.

"She was hurt, but it could've been worse. Maybe she should learn not to try to take on demons twice her size," I muttered. "They won't get to her again, I can promise you that."

The painting rattled harder, and a couple of kitchen cabinets opened.

"You don't believe me?"

One of the cabinet doors shut, then opened again.

"I don't need to be lectured by a ghost," I grunted, searching for a coffee mug while more cabinet doors shook around me. "You're as bad as the rest of them. Not understanding. And I'm not about to explain myself to you." I sighed, resting my hands on the counter and hanging my head. "Great, now I'm losing it and talking to a ghost."

Something pinched the back of my arm, and I flinched with a growl.

"What do you want me to say, huh? What?"

The bag of coffee grounds I'd left out tipped and spilled over. I started to reach out to wipe them up but paused. The word truth was spelled out, and I shook my head.

"Truth about what?"

An arrow appeared beneath the word, pointing toward the bedroom.

"The truth is complicated, just like having a relationship with me would be complicated. And dangerous, and I can't put Cara through heartbreak like that. Not when—" I cut myself off, not letting the word leave my mouth. "The last time I trusted someone so openly, I nearly lost everything," I admitted quietly. "It's not that I think Cara would ever do the same to me. She's got a good heart, and that's the problem. If I give in to what we both want, there's no going back. I can't lose again, and I especially can't lose her. Is that good enough for you?"

Beth pinched the back of my arm again, and I snarled, swiping my arm behind me to chase the spirit away. The chill that had been in the air evaporated, and I knew I was alone again.

Except I wasn't.

Cara was just down the hall. It'd been easier to keep my distance when I wasn't staying in her house with her. Now, her scent surrounded me in every room, and I could picture her at the kitchen counter. See her sitting in the living room, lounging on the couch. The ghost of her laughter followed me around while I searched for tools to fix the sink and whatever other odd jobs I could find to work on. I chugged a mug of steaming hot coffee, hoping the slight burn would ground me. Every minute, I fought against the desire to traipse through the house and be with her. One kiss was all it had taken to destroy months of hard-built resolve.

Had it been like this for Arkon? Or for Dagon? They'd told me how intense the emotional connection became once they admitted the truth to themselves, but I never expected it to make me feel like I was being torn apart, not being by her side. Not seeing her or touching her. My chest ached, and I hadn't stopped growling for the last hour or so.

THE NIGHT SKY had given way to an overcast morning. I was wedged under the kitchen sink again, cursing at the pipes.

The air shifted around me.

I jerked upright, smashing my head on the underside of the counter with a snarl.

"Shit, my fault," Cara said, crouching beside the sink and grimacing at me. "You alright?"

"Fantastic," I bit out. I shifted forward, so I was out in the open, holding my hand to my sore forehead. Her soft scent surrounded me, and my hand itched to touch her. My gaze shifted, taking in the bruises on her neck and jaw, courtesy of last night's brawl. I growled, imagining burning those two assholes to death all over again for hurting her.

"I'm alright," she murmured. "They don't hurt that bad."

My hands grew hot, and I struggled to keep my fire under control. Flames sparked at my hands, and she studied them with a curious glint in her eyes. "It won't hurt you," I said, the words coming out stiff. "The fire."

"I wasn't worried it would." She offered me a smile, then cleared her throat, nodding to the sink behind me. "You don't have to do that, you know."

"Had to do something to keep myself busy."

"How long have you been awake?" she asked, then her eyes shimmered with concern. "Did you even go to sleep?"

"Not the first time I've gone without it."

"I'm sure it's not. You up for some breakfast? I make a mean omelet."

She hadn't moved away from me yet, and I was too distracted by how little she wore to answer. The tank top she had on hid nothing, nor did the skimpy cotton shorts that rode high up her thighs. Gods, the curves on this woman alone drove me mad most days when she wore jeans. Now, I could see so much skin my imagination took off. It wouldn't take much to have her naked.

The kitchen wasn't ideal, but rational thought wasn't exactly working for me right then. Her chest rose and fell quickly with her breathing. Those mounds caught my eye, her nipples hardening beneath the thin layer of fabric. If she leaned over any further, I wouldn't be able to control myself. My hands warmed, and I started to shift away until her hand stretched up. She pressed her fingers to my sore forehead, and every muscle in my body tensed.

Her brow crinkled. "You want some ice for this?"

I tried to speak, but all that came out of my mouth was a strained, incoherent mumble in demonic. Her scent wrapped around me. She might not have fire burning in her veins, but she was warm to me all the same. Her lively presence sparked a different type of blaze deep in my soul. I shut my eyes, trying to find a way to tell her this had to stop before it went too far. She held my face in her palms and pressed her lips to mine so tenderly at first, then more demanding while her fingers dove into my hair. I hauled her onto my lap the next second, crushing her to me while her lips parted on a quiet moan. Squeezing her ass, I bucked my hips, hating there were too many barriers between me and what was mine.

She wound her arms around my neck, pressing those pert nipples right into me. My hands wanted to be everywhere at once. They held her ass, then massaged up her thighs until I snagged her hips. Our lips never parted, and the idea of taking her right there on the damn floor sounded like an option. The life burning within her chased away the dark cloud that had followed me around for years. She transported me out of the demon I'd let myself become and straight into the one I never thought I could be.

But maybe with Cara, it was possible.

I slid the strap of her tank top down, trailing kisses down her neck then to the smooth skin of her shoulder. She gripped my horns, gently rocking her hips against my swollen shaft. Lightly, I dragged my claws down her bareback, and she shivered. Worried I'd scared her, I raised my head to find her eyes hooded with want and her nibbling her lip.

"You know there's a bed just down the hall," she murmured, her voice husky.

Instinct raged for me to pick her up and carry her off to finally have her.

"Calrod?" she asked, her eyes searching.

I sighed, picking up a lock of her hair and letting it fall through my fingers. I started to speak, but she covered my mouth with her hand. The sad smile she gave me spoke volumes without her saying a damn word. She kissed my cheek, climbed off my lap, and walked away. Not stormed off, or cursed me out, just simply walked away as if we hadn't been a few heated minutes away from tearing each other's clothes off and going at it.

I knocked my head on the cabinets, cursing the fates for sending me to Cara, then went back to fixing the sink. Cara's scent lingered, as did her touch. I managed to get the sink fixed and put back together in less than an hour. I was coming in from the laundry room after returning the tools and spotted Cara snagging a thermos of coffee. She picked her apron off the hook by the garage door.

"I'm going to be out there if you need anything," she said with a bright smile.

"In the garage?" I'd never actually been out there in all the times I'd been to her house. I'd been curious but hadn't wanted to pry.

"Yeah, figured it was safe. Still part of the house, and since Jasmine just texted me in all caps saying I wasn't allowed to come to work today, I figured I'd get something accomplished." She came to me, stood on her toes, and lightly kissed my lips. "You're more than welcome to join me if you want."

"I'll let you have some space," I murmured.

"Fine, but we're not going to lie to each other anymore about what this is. Nothing's going to change that." She headed out the door, leaving me in the kitchen even more confused than I was last night, seeing her reaction to me being a demon.

I wasn't sure what I was going to do all day. Leaving wasn't an option, not until the warding was in place and we knew it worked. Sipping on a cup of coffee, I meandered around Cara's cottage. There wasn't much else to fix, and after twenty minutes, I decided to join her in the garage. She sat in the center of the space, a pottery wheel in front of her. She glanced at me over her shoulder and grinned.

"There's a chair somewhere out here if you want it."

Absently, I nodded, my gaze roaming over the shelves filled with unpainted pottery, some finished pieces and others wrapped in layers of thick plastic. "You made all this?"

"Yep. Hobby of mine."

"Do you sell these pieces anywhere?" I spun around, watching her clay-covered hands work on a new piece while the wheel turned.

"I do craft fairs every now and then. A lot of people in town ask me for special pieces sometimes. That's about it." She tilted her head, shaping the clay into a taller column.

Unlike at the shop when she was setting up new items, here, her eyes glimmered with a creative light

I hadn't noticed before. It was impossible not to watch her work, see the clay take form beneath her hands. She appeared utterly relaxed, as if demons hadn't tried to murder her last night or that she hadn't been told another demon was her mate. Or that magic existed.

"How do you do it?" I blurted.

"Do what?" she asked, not looking up.

"Not completely lose your mind with what was dumped on you last night."

"Like it told you, I learned to deal." She said it with a smile, but a flicker of doubt crept onto her face, breaking her concentration. She sighed at the clay that had shifted. Smashing it down, she mumbled under her breath about starting over.

I knew she'd been lying this whole time, putting on a mask and pretending she had nerves made of steel. Going to her and comforting her would've been the thing to do if I was willing to accept we were mates. But Carridan was still out there. I had to stay focused, which meant I had to do precisely what she didn't want.

Pretend there was nothing between us.

A car pulled up, and I tensed with a growl. Dagon's Tahoe parked behind Cara's hatchback, and Morgan climbed out from behind the wheel, waving.

"I come bearing gifts from Cyrene," she announced once she'd joined us in the garage. "And instructions for you, Calrod. How you doing?" she asked Cara.

"I'm doing just fine. You and Jasmine can stop asking me that any time now."

Morgan's eyes narrowed, and her smile faltered. Then it was right back on her face. "Just have to ask, and she's pregnant. Her hormones are bouncing all over the place, so she's in panic mode about every-thing right now."

"Is she at the shop?" Cara asked.

"No, Arkon convinced her to stay home for the day. I would've gone in, but I was with Cyrene all night and this morning." She yawned, shaking out her head. "Shop's just closed for the day. Man, you have any coffee left?"

Cara made to stand, but I waved her off. "I can do it. You said you have instructions for me anyway, right?"

"Sure do." Morgan followed me into the house. I left the garage door cracked, so I could hear and keep an eye on Cara. "Aren't you just full of smiles and sunshine today."

"Long night," I grunted. Satisfied nothing was going to try and kill Cara in the next five minutes, I scrounged around for another mug and poured it full for Morgan. "What did Cyrene send you with?"

"Protective charms for you both to wear and more to bury around the cottage. Dagon's at your place burying some others there."

"What about the warding around the town?" I took the bag Morgan offered, removing two tiny black bottles hanging from silver chains. There were four heavy sachets with them, each one marked with a different symbol representing the elements.

"Still working on it. Cyrene's pissed it failed the first time. She's trying to come up with something that packs more of a punch. Think of these as until we get it up and in case it fails." She gave me instructions on how and where to bury them to ensure they were effective. She fell silent afterward, but her eyes were far from quiet.

"I know you want to say something else, so get it over with."

She looked to the door, but Cara was still working away at the pottery wheel. "Where do you want me to start? Her, or you?"

"I'm not the one who just had a brush with death."

"Great, I'll start with Cara." Morgan planted her hands on her hips. "You're an idiot if you think she's handling all of this alright. She's not, not even close. Jasmine's been freaking out about her all night and this morning. Apparently, it's one of Cara's great tricks, putting on a smile. She acted the same way when she went through some shit a couple years back."

"What was it?"

"Nope, that's for you to ask her. What I will tell you is all this nonsense about you keeping your distance from her to keep her safe is only going to make it harder on her to get through whatever comes next," Morgan said, poking me in the chest. "You might be able to hide thoughts from Dagon, but you can't hide your emotions, not from me. Your energy has been gloomy since the first time I saw you."

"Gloomy?" I scoffed. "Then you read me wrong."

"Not possible. You're hiding some big dark secret. Carrying around guilt that I don't understand, and frankly, it's not for me to get into. That's something you should be talking about with that woman out there."

"I'm not hiding anything."

"None of you can lie at all. You certainly can't lie to someone who can read energies and emotions," she said, emphasizing the last few words.

"Just drop it, alright?" I snapped. "You gave me the charms. You can go."

"Oh, I'm going, but you're going to stop keeping your brothers and your mate at arm's length. Say it aloud, and maybe you'll stop trying to deny what's right in front of your face. If you don't, she's not going to be the only one suffering."

"Maybe it's what I deserve," I blurted.

"For what?"

I growled, wanting her to leave already.

"You don't want to tell me, fine. But you can't keep the past hidden forever, and Cara needs you, just as much as you need her." She gave my arm a squeeze on her way out of the kitchen. "Take a note from your brothers. They tried to fight it, too, but look how much stronger we are together?"

"Great, I can claim Cara as mine right before Carridan shows up to kill her."

"No one's seen that outcome, as far as I know." She looked like she wanted to say more but told me to take care of the sachets, make sure Cara got the protection charm and promised she'd be in touch with any news.

From where I stood in the kitchen, I heard Morgan talking to Cara for a few minutes. Then she was pulling away from the house. I peered through the crack in the garage door, my heart lurching. Cara was hunched over the pottery wheel, holding her head. She sniffed hard, shook out her arms, and went right back to working the clay as if she wasn't on the verge of having a breakdown. Wondering what Morgan meant when she said Cara had gone through something, I backed away from the door. I wasn't ready to come clean about a past I'd tried to keep buried. Still, each time I kissed Cara, being so close to her this long made it clear how impossible staying away would be.

Then were other concerns to take into consideration. Even if I stepped out of her life, her ability to speak to the dead and Cyrene's warning about what that could lead to remained. Cara couldn't go back to how her life was before. I cursed Cyrene again for saying anything in the first place. And for lying to us again. I wasn't the only one who had secrets. I sensed the ones Cyrene held close were far worse than mine.

"So, what do you do?" I muttered to myself while I looked at the garage door. "Protect her from afar? Watch over her for the rest of her life while you slink back into the shadows?" I had no good choices, none that would ensure Cara would be safe.

Hoping I wasn't going to add another regret to my already long list, I made my decision.

LATER THAT AFTERNOON, after the sachets had been buried, I finally went out to the garage to check on Cara. I'd spent most of the day alone with my thoughts, weighing the chances that giving in would lead to tragedy. I'd been on my own for so long, the idea of being with someone who was quickly bringing me back to life was exhilarating and terrifying at the same time. So many things could go wrong.

And yet, no matter how much I tried to deny it, fully giving myself to Cara and being with her would be worth it.

Quietly, I stepped into the garage and stilled. Cara picked up the hunk of clay that had been an almost finished project and chucked it out of the garage. Cursing, she scraped her fingers across the wheel, pulling more chunks of clay free and throwing them, too. When she finished, she whipped around and froze.

"Calrod?" She quickly turned away, wiping at her face with a clean corner of her apron. "I didn't hear you come out. Everything okay?" She sniffed a few times.

"Fine. The charms are buried."

"Good, that's good. Thanks for taking care of that. And don't worry, I'm still wearing my necklace."

I'd brought it out to her on my way to bury the charms around the property. She'd had that same fake cheery smile on her face, then too. Now, however, her eyes were red like she'd been crying. It had to be because of me. Guilt gnawed at me, as did Morgan's warning.

"Why don't you come inside for a bit? I thought I'd make something for dinner."

"Is it that late already?"

"Close enough. You haven't eaten all day, and neither have I."

"I can order take out," she said. "Haven't been to the store in a while."

"I'll take care of it." I rubbed the back of my neck, unsure what to say.

Cara held up her hands, looking at them, then at the clay she'd launched out of the garage. "I should clean all this up first."

"I can manage. Go take a nice hot shower. Relax for a bit."

She picked at the clay bits on her hands but

nodded. "If you're sure. Shower would probably be a good idea." She pulled her apron off, draped it over the stool she'd been sitting on, and hurried past me and inside.

Once she was gone, I cleaned up the pottery wheel the best I could. The clay on the driveway wasn't worth saving, so I tossed it in the trashcan. That finished, I closed the garage and made a call to the local diner for a delivery order. From the kitchen, I was able to hear the shower running, and I found myself pacing from one end of the hall to the other, driven by an instinctual need to be close to her. The burgers and fries I'd ordered, along with a couple of apple pie slices, arrived about half an hour later. I put on my glamour long enough to answer the door, then let it fall once I was back in the kitchen. The shower had shut off a while ago, but Cara hadn't emerged from her room. It gave me a chance to set the food out and my nerves to fray even more.

Getting ready to admit the truth was a hell of a lot harder than I thought it'd be. I'd never felt so raw and confused by what was happening to my soul. Nothing made sense as much as it did at the same time. I grunted, wondering if I should've talked to my brothers first. Get some sort of advice from them on how to handle this situation.

A door opened, and Cara appeared in the double doorway of the kitchen bundled in an oversized green sweater that hung off her right shoulder. She had denim shorts on and was barefoot. Her hair was even curlier from the shower. There was no redness around her eyes, so she hadn't been crying.

"Nothing like seeing a demon standing in your kitchen," she said quietly.

"I can put the glamour back," I reminded her, but she held up her hand.

"I don't want that. Seeing you like this, it doesn't scare me." She laughed, murmuring, "I've honestly never felt safer or normal if that makes any sense at all."

"I guess I'm still in shock you're not trying to throw something at me." I smiled, hoping it'd lighten the tension that had flooded the kitchen. Instead, Cara's eyes glistened with emotion, and she shoved her hands in her butt pockets, avoiding my gaze. "It's alright to be afraid, you know, of all this. No one's expecting you to be okay with anything. Falling apart is completely acceptable."

"I don't know if that's what this is." She shrugged, wandering into the kitchen. "I'm so worried about Jasmine and the baby and Arkon. They're all so happy. Even Dagon and Morgan, then there's you, and I just can't stop thinking about how wrong this can all go."

"You didn't mention yourself in there," I pointed out.

"I'm not scared for myself," she said. "I mean, yeah, nearly dying is terrifying, I guess, but somehow that doesn't frighten me. Kind of been around death all my life."

I growled, not sure I liked the tone this conversation was taking.

She frowned, then shook her head, walking around the table until she stood right in front of me. "I'm not saying I want to die or anything. Sorry, this is all coming out wrong." She pressed her hand to her chest, her face scrunching so much it had to hurt. The bruise that had been on her jaw this morning had darkened, as had the ones around her neck. I wondered how she wasn't more concerned about her own safety. "I know you want to act like we're not what we are to one another, but I haven't been scared of anything since the day I met you. That sounds ridiculous, and I was never one of those women who believed in love at first sight or whatever, but," she puffed out her cheeks and threw her head back. "Damn, alright, I'm just going to say this, and I'm probably going to mess it up. I was with another guy for a long time, and I thought he was it."

My growl deepened, and I wondered how hard it'd be to track down this man and ensure he never came near Cara again.

"You can calm down. Haven't talked to him in years," she assured me. "While I was with him, things were good, but it never fit right. I never fully trusted him, then he ended up cheating on me, and it was a whole thing," she rambled. "Messed me up for a few years."

"None of what you're saying makes sense yet. You know that, right?"

She rolled her eyes, then grabbed ahold of my arms. "I know, just bear with me here. What I'm trying to tell you is what I felt with him, it doesn't even come close to what I've felt for you this entire time. And hearing Cyrene and the others tell me why that is, it just made it all real. Made me less worried it was all inside my head. Now, though, I'm worried I might've pushed too hard, and I'm sorry for that. I get how it might not be easy to deal with the truth being thrown at you, but there you go."

"That's what's got you so worked up?" I whispered in disbelief. "Cara, I've been terrified this whole time that you'd see my true face and hate me."

"Why?"

I blinked, disbelieving how accepting this woman was. "The demon thing. Most normal people run the other direction and don't look back."

"Unless they're meant to be together," she whispered with a small smile.

"We haven't even gone on a date yet. Hell, you don't even know me, not really. Most of what I told you were the same lies that I tell everyone. Can't exactly go around describing the Underworld to humans."

"Well, good thing you're not going anywhere. We'll just have to redo every conversation." She started to walk away, but I caught her hands, pulling her right back to me.

I licked my lips, unable to stop the blue flames that crackled to life in my palms and spread toward her. The fire reflected in her fascinated gaze. It caressed her hands and longed to go further, but I held it back. "For the record, you're not pushing too hard. I never expected to find, well, you. Told myself I didn't need someone."

"You've never felt like this for anyone before?"

No holding back. No more pretending. If I was doing this, I was going all in. I wound my arm around her waist, the fire following my lead, and lowered my mouth, whispering, "Demons mate for life, Cara. You're the only woman I've ever burned for."

I let her close the distance. The kiss was sweet and far too short, but there was so much we needed to figure out. I drew back, loving how she licked her lips immediately after and grinned.

I expected the conversation to be awkward, but I should've known better. Once we sat down and started talking, we never stopped. A couple of hours later, we'd migrated from the kitchen to her bedroom. I'd hesitated in the doorway, but she'd raised her brow at me and patted the bed beside her. We'd brought in a few beers and picked up our conversation where we left off. She'd told me more about her life growing up and learning she could see and talk to the dead. I described the Under-world, more about demons and our nature, and about my family until it all fell apart. I stumbled over my words a few times, doing my best to give her the truth as much as possible. Each time, she'd take my hand, quietly telling me again we didn't have to go over everything tonight. One of these days, she'd learn the whole truth. Would she feel the same for me then? Knowing what I'd let happen because I'd been blinded by what I thought was love? Her ex had merely cheated on her.

Mine had caused the deaths of my parents and me and my brothers being exiled.

We sat with our backs to the wooden headboard. The conversation had come to a natural stopping point. For the most part, I felt less stressed, but we'd avoided discussing Carridan in-depth or Cyrene's plans for Cara. Or the possibility of when our world would come crashing down around us.

"Is this weird to you?" she asked.

"Is what weird?"

"You came to Oak Hollow to help your brother and his girlfriend, then bam! You find me, your mate. I mean, what are the chances of that. And here we are months later, and it's just, I don't know."

"If you're worried about this happening too fast," I started, but she laughed. "What?"

"Too fast? You're joking. You and I have been dancing around asking each other out for way too damn long. This right here feels like I'm waking up from a dream. The second I saw you without your glamour, that was when I woke up. It's almost like the last few months of not being this close to you don't even exist." Her smile faltered, and she asked in a rush, "Unless it's too fast for you?"

I took her hand and kissed the back of it. Her eyes glimmered, and she relaxed against the pillows. "Not even close."

"So you're admitting it then?"

I mulled over the words I could say, then figured actions were far louder. I captured her mouth in a kiss, languidly stroking her tongue with mine, coaxing a moan from her. She wrapped her leg around mine, snuggling closer. More of the dark shadow I'd held in my heart all these years dissipated thanks to the woman held fast in my arms. Cara stifled a yawn, and I smoothed her hair from her forehead, planting a kiss there.

"You should get some sleep."

"Don't need it. Wide awake," she argued, then yawned again.

"Sleep." I moved to go, but she held onto me.

"Stay with me, 'til I fall pass out at least?"

"Whatever you need," I promised, sensing the weight behind my words. From the way she looked up at me, the same promise in her eyes, she felt it, too.

I dragged the quilts up the bed, tucked her in against my chest, and counted off the seconds while she fell asleep. It took less than two minutes, and she was out. I thought about leaving her be, but the idea of moving right then made my stomach twist.

"No more fighting it," I whispered to the night. "Just don't let me lose her. Please, gods, don't let me lose her."

6

———

Cara

I dropped another armful of books and cursed.

"You didn't have to come in today," Jasmine called from the counter in the center of the shop.

"And what else was I going to do?" I scooped up the hardbacks and carried them to where she worked, sitting on a tall, cushy stool Arkon had bought for her a few weeks back. "Calrod's with Dagon scoping out the town to see if any more of Carridan's bloodhounds are here. And Morgan's with Cyrene working on the warding with those witches who came to town. We both know Calrod wasn't going to let me stay home alone."

"She's got a point," Arkon said from behind a set of wooden shelves before Jasmine could reply.

"You three can't put us on lockdown every time something happens."

Arkon barked a laugh. "How many times do I have to tell you, Jas?"

"Yeah, yeah, demons are protective of what's theirs and possessive and ungodly annoying about all of it." He poked his head around the shelves, his glamour down for the moment, and she beamed at him. "I love you."

He grunted and went back to arranging the box of trinkets she'd given him to set out. When he finished, she sent him to the back to sort through a few items that may or may not have magical properties. She'd picked up a shipment from an estate up north, a house I'd helpfully told her a few weeks back was supposed to be haunted. After what she'd found from the last place that had been owned by a witch, Arkon wasn't keen on letting her near any of it until he looked at it first.

"Right, spill," Jasmine whispered the second Arkon was out of sight.

"About what?"

"What do you think? Calrod spent the last two nights at your place." She wiggled her brow, nudging me. "Come on, you can't tell me you two haven't been getting it on."

"Pregnancy makes you so freaking horny."

"Could be worse." She nudged me again, grinning.

"We haven't had sex if that's what you're really wanting to know," I whispered, watching the backroom closely in case Arkon popped out. "I mean, there's been some pretty heated kissing and snuggling must run in the family because damn. I've never slept so well in my life."

I'd fallen asleep with Calrod holding me, and that was exactly how I'd awakened. Each time I'd shifted, he'd moved with me, keeping us together through the night and into the morning. I'd never thought simply sleeping with someone could be so relaxing and heated, and man, if I didn't have sexy dreams all night long because of it.

"You sure you didn't do anything else?" Jasmine asked. "Your face is on fire right now."

"I might've had a dream or two, but no, just kissing." My lips tingled while they remembered the embrace Calrod had left me with after bringing me here. "We spent most of last night talking."

"Those are good moments, too," Jasmine agreed, glancing toward the back of the shop. "Arkon and

Dagon, they've been worried about Calrod for a while now."

"I can see why. He carries sadness around him like a second skin."

"You noticed that, too, huh?"

"Hard not to. From what he's said, sounds as if he never expected to find happiness, especially with someone like me. Guess he thought he'd be alone for the rest of his life."

"But now he won't be. He's better around you," she said, pushing aside a stack of books to start labeling the next ones. "I noticed it the first time he came to the shop with you here. That was back when my life was in danger the last year."

"Explains why he was distant then." I opened my mouth but shut it. Whatever secrets Calrod had, I sensed they were going to take time to unravel. And something told me the reason for his guilt and sorrow wasn't known by his brothers. The last thing he needed was Jasmine bugging him with her lack of filter. "I think he's still worried about all of this, but we had a breakthrough last night, I think."

"Yeah?"

"He's still waiting for me to have a mental breakdown, though."

"He's not the only one."

I sighed, turning to look at Jasmine attempting to keep her eyes focused on the leatherbound black book in front of her. "I'm not about to fall apart over here. Like I told you guys, learning all of this is real is comforting in a way. Wasn't it the same for you?"

"In a way, but I'd already seen a demon. You just see..." She failed to get the words out, and I laughed.

"Dead people, Jas. I see dead people, several of whom are currently in your shop right now."

"Don't tell me that. Now I'm going to be paranoid they're watching me." Her eyes bugged, and she groaned, covering her face with her hands. "Shit. We've had sex in this shop."

I laughed. "From what I can tell, most spirits don't pry into personal moments. Sure you're safe."

She looked around the shop, but the man in the top hat and the other women who'd shown up the same time he did weren't visible to me right then. Jasmine shook her head, then swiveled the stool around to face me. "You're really okay with all of this?" she asked and took hold of my hand.

I covered her hand with my free one. "For the hundredth time, yes, it's a lot take in, but I'm processing, and I'm good. It's funny, really. The questions I've had about what else might be out there instead of just ghosts got answered in one night. Kinda nice, really. Saved me some research time."

"You're insane."

"Right back at ya."

She rolled her eyes, then hugged me as much as she could with her rounded belly.

"Now, can we stop worrying about me and get back to focusing on you and the baby?" She took my hand and placed it on the side of her belly. A kick came a second later, and I laughed, staring in disbelief. "I'm so happy for you."

"Me too," she replied, wiping at her eyes. "Damn hormones."

"But you're good otherwise? The stress isn't getting to you?"

Jasmine dabbed at her eyes with a tissue she yanked from the nearby box. "I might've been a mess after we left your house. I was doing so good for those first couple of weeks after Dagon had his vision, but seeing those demons here makes the danger Arkon always warned me about so freaking real."

"He won't let anything happen to you or the baby."

"I know, but that means he'll be putting himself in the line of fire to save us." She held her stomach, tears slipping down her cheeks. "I can't do this without him. We just found each other, you know?" She laughed, wiping at her face with the fresh tissue I handed her. "Shit, listen to me. Course you know. You just found Calrod."

I hugged her again, trying not to let her see how worried I was that this Prince Carridan jackass was going to show up at the worst possible time. But I'd seen Calrod fight, and I heard the stories of what Dagon and Arkon had done to keep the people they loved safe.

"It's going to work out," I promised, not sure why my words sounded so empty.

I'd jumped headfirst into the deep end, entering a world I was still attempting to comprehend. Calrod had told me a couple of times how dangerous my life was going to be if we were together. I might not fully understand just how bad it could get yet, but I did know the notion of not seeing Calrod again or touching him left a hole in the pit of my stomach. I spent years wondering why I felt alone even when I was with friends, or the boyfriend I thought loved me, or hell, all the spirits I'd roomed with. Now I realized I was waiting for a brooding demon to walk into my life. I hadn't lied when I told him how everything felt like a dream before these last couple of days. A long-ass dream I'd worried wasn't going to end.

I was going to tell Jasmine a bit more about what had gone on between Calrod and me, figuring she needed the distraction, but a flash out of the corner of my eye caught my attention.

"Cara?" Jasmine asked. "You alright?"

The spirits who had been quiet all day appeared near the front door of the shop. The two women were peering out the window, rapidly shimmering in and out of view. Usually, that meant they were agitated. Then Mr. Top Hat waved his arm over his head, looking right at me. What were they doing?

"Cara?"

"Yeah, uh, sorry, the ghosts are being weird," I told Jasmine.

"They can be weird?"

Making my way around the counter, I nodded. Mr. Top Hat was still waving his arm over his head, then pointing out the window. His lips were moving, but like most spirits I encountered, no sound came out. I had no idea what he was trying to tell me. A vase flew across the shop, shattering against the wall.

Jasmine cursed, and Arkon came running.

"What was that?" he demanded in a growl.

"Ghost, I think," Jasmine replied.

"I don't know what they're doing," I said over my shoulder. "They're freaking out about something."

"Can you find out what?" Arkon snapped.

I didn't let his anger bother me, not when he was merely protecting Jasmine. I walked to the ghosts, peering out the window they were so focused on. There weren't any other cars in the parking lot aside from Jasmine's Jeep and my hatchback. I was about to tell them that, but a sudden chill stole the air from my lungs. I doubled over, gasping, and the room spun.

My mouth opened, and a voice that wasn't mine came out.

"Darkness. It's coming," a deep male warned. "We feel it, the power. Danger. He brings danger and death. Run, you have to run—" the voice cut off, and I was left coughing.

I fell to my knees, a shiver passing through me.

"Seriously?" I coughed a few more times, glaring at the ghost in the top hat. "Warn me next time."

"Did you just get possessed?" Jasmine exclaimed.

"Briefly. Happens sometimes, but it's rare." I made it to my feet and peered out the window, the ghost's words coming back to me. "We should go, like right now."

Arkon took Jasmine's hand, ignoring her questions, and guided her to the front door. I kept a watch outside, but no cars pulled up, and I didn't see any demons charging up the gravel drive leading to the shop. I kept waiting for the protective charms we wore to activate. If this evil presence was this close, they'd let us know, wouldn't they? Once Arkon and Jasmine were with me, I opened the front door, and it slammed shut right in my face. I yanked on the knob, but it refused to budge. I glanced up, confused. The three spirits were doing everything they could to keep us inside.

"Make up your minds," I yelled. "You want us to leave or stay?"

Mr. Top Hat was shaking his head and pointing outside again.

"What are they saying?" Arkon asked, his body shifting right before my eyes.

It was like watching Calrod charging into my house to fight those demons all over again. Seeing the demon come out would never not fascinate me, the sight of the predator being fully unleashed.

"Cara." Arkon's tone was quite aggravated. Clearly, with me.

"Right, sorry. I think whatever's coming is already here." As if waiting for me to speak, the small, black jar warmed against my skin in warning.

I pulled it out of my shirt to see it pulsing with a bright, violet light. I waited for them to do something, make a shield or something. The light pulsed faster coming from all three charms. It became blinding, then the jars shattered, taking the light with them.

"Shit."

"Call Calrod," Arkon ordered. "And you two are going to lock yourselves in the backroom. Now."

Jasmine hesitated, but his eyes shimmered, and she dragged him to her by his shirt, kissed him, and stormed off.

I was right behind her, calling Calrod while we wound our way through the shop to the backroom. We locked the doors behind us, and Jasmine opened a locked cabinet, pulled out a shotgun, and proceeded to load it. Good thing we both knew how to shoot. I double-checked the rear doors were bolted. Thanks to the attack that occurred here last year, Arkon had put in heavily reinforced ones that weren't merely physically locked but magically locked, too. Nothing was coming in that way.

Calrod's phone went to voicemail both times I called.

On the third, I left him a message saying something was wrong at the shop. Halfway through the message, there was a click. I answered.

"Cara?"

"We've got trouble," I told Calrod. "Where are you?"

"On our way back to the shop. What's wrong?"

"I don't know. The ghosts started acting all weird, wanting us to leave then not wanting us to leave. The protection charms exploded. We barricaded ourselves in the back, and Arkon went outside."

Dagon cursed in the background. "We'll be there in ten," he yelled into the phone.

"I'm sure it's nothing to worry about," I said, trying to keep my tone light.

Calrod's answering growl said I did a horrible job of it. "You stay in that damn room, understand? Do not go out there. Arkon can handle himself."

I glanced to Jasmine, clutching the shotgun in her white-knuckled grip and staring at the doors leading into the shop. That was her mate out there, the father of her child. Could I really just sit here and what, listen to Arkon potentially get killed?

"Cara," Calrod said loudly. "Did you hear me?"

"Just get here fast as you can," I said and hung up, cutting off his curse. "Ten minutes out. Give me that, and you sit down on the couch and try to relax."

Jasmine gave me the shotgun but stayed standing. "We don't even know what's out there."

"Arkon's a hardass. Nothing's going to hurt him."

The bell at the front of the shop tinkled, and we sucked in a collective breath. I leveled the gun at the doors, waiting for Arkon to give the all-clear.

A knock came a few seconds later, followed by his voice.

I started to lower the gun, but Jasmine snagged my shoulder.

"That's not Arkon," she whispered.

"Jasmine?" A second knock came at the door. "It's safe. Open the door."

My finger inched toward the trigger, praying Jasmine was right. Mr. Top Hat appeared suddenly to my left, and I jumped, quietly cursing him out. He pointed at the door, shaking his head, then mimed me shooting. Great, if that wasn't Arkon, then where the hell was he?

The not-Arkon knocked harder, demanding we open the door and let him in. I motioned for Jasmine to stand back in the corner, adjusted my feet, and let out a shaky breath. With the help of the ghost, I shifted my aim and squeezed the trigger. The blast struck the door but didn't go all the way through. The person on the side shouted. Ignoring him, I cocked the gun and fired a second time. A man cursed, followed by a crash of wood and glass.

"You fucking bitch," he snarled. "Damn it. Look at what you did to me."

"Stay here," I told Jasmine and went to the door, peering through the holes I'd created.

A man who was clearly not Arkon, nor a demon, lay on the floor, his front bloody. He gasped, struggling to get air. I kept the barrel trained on him, wondering where the real Arkon was. The front door flew open not long after, and my question was answered.

Arkon hauled the intruder up by his shirt and slammed him into the nearest bookshelf, roaring furiously in his face.

The man sputtered, blood covering his lips, then he shuddered and went limp. Arkon tossed him aside, his amber eyes flicking to the door.

"Safe," he said, the word barely audible beneath the growling.

I hurried to unlock the doors, and Jasmine rushed out and straight into his arms. He hugged her, his face and body adjusting while the demon rage slipped away.

"Where the hell were you?" Jasmine yelled. "I thought you were dead."

"There were three more outside waiting," he explained, kissing the top of her head. "I'm sorry."

"What are they?" I asked, keeping the shotgun aimed at the body a few yards away. The horrible notion struck me that I'd just murdered someone, and my stomach roiled. I'd attacked the demons in my house, but this guy, I was pretty sure even without Arkon's help, the gunshot wounds would've sent him to the afterlife.

"Witches. The ones outside are alive, though I'm sure they wish they weren't," Arkon said, his tone filled with malice. "Cara, you did what you had to do," he added sternly. "Don't let it get to you."

"Bit late for that," I muttered and let out a shaky breath. "I'm alright. Everything's fine."

"How did they get so close?" Jasmine asked.

"They spoofed their way past the warding," Arkon replied. "A spell probably broke the protection charms."

"How do you spoof your way around warding?" Jasmine demanded furiously.

"No idea, but I'd like to find out. We need to get them to Cyrene, all of them."

We'd just dragged the dead witch outside, then Calrod and Dagon showed up. Calrod's eyes flared blue, and he looked more than ready to lose it.

Arkon snapped his name, and the brothers spoke quietly in that damn language I really needed to learn. Dagon joined them. Whatever he said set Calrod off. He shoved his youngest brother and stormed off to the three witches who'd survived Arkon's assault. None of them were conscious yet, and from the murderous glint in Calrod's narrowed eyes, he was about to ensure that was permanent.

The glimmer of fear I caught in his gaze next drew me to him. I slipped my hand into his heated one. He flinched, and I held on tighter. His palm warmed even more in my grip. "Don't," he bit off.

"Don't what? Let you know I'm okay?"

His hand went from warm to burning hot. He broke free, and I spotted the tiny flame forming in his palm until he closed his fist around it, snuffing out the fire. "We can talk about this later."

"Yeah? Why do I get the feeling that's a later that'll never happen?"

"We need to get these witches to Cyrene's place," he said quietly, avoiding my gaze, and stormed away.

I considered following, remembering what he'd said last night. He hadn't thought I was pushing him to accept what I was to him. After this, though, I wasn't sure he'd feel the same if I kept at it. Jasmine appeared at my side, linking her arm through mine.

"He'll be alright," she said. "Not sure what it is about them, but none of them could simply accept the truth at first."

"Stubborn ass men," I said, and Jasmine laughed.

"Something like that. Come on. The faster we get to Cyrene's place, the faster we can get our lectures over with. You're not the only one who's probably going to get one. You sure you're ready to be with a demon for life?" she asked with a teasing glance.

I caught Calrod's eye, and he stilled. Flames erupted in his hands, and the bluish aura I'd started to notice more easily around him glowed for a brief second.

"I'm not sure he's ready to be with anyone for life," I replied sadly.

So much for having a breakthrough. I sighed, then walked with Jasmine to join the others and head over to Cyrene's house with our prisoners and dead in tow.

Calrod parked my hatchback in the drive and turned it off. There'd been no conversation on the way home from Cyrene's place. Despite what I'd assumed would happen once we were there, I hadn't received any sort of lecture or talk from him. He'd hardly spoken to me directly during the entire five hours we were there with the others.

Jasmine had barely been able to calm Arkon down. After she had, he hadn't let go of her hand for a second. They'd gone off to another room to talk. That talk turned into them yelling at each other about being reckless. By the time they'd come back, they had one arm wrapped around the other and were grinning like idiots. This love-mate bond thing was a strange creature, that I had no doubts about at all.

Cyrene had examined the witches. The three alive ones had regained consciousness. None of them were willing to speak, but they didn't have to. She'd figured out how they'd managed to spoof their way past the warding. They'd gotten their hands on some of Arkon's DNA. It hadn't taken much. A couple of hairs had done the trick, along with a potent spell and some other stuff Cyrene had rattled off that I hadn't understood. That was also how they'd destroyed the charms she'd made to keep us safe. The point was that Cyrene's concern had been that no warding she or the others placed around Oak Hollow would keep Carridan from reaching any of us.

And that had been the first thing to make Calrod's hackles rise. The second had been when Arkon told him how I'd become possessed by spirits. Cyrene had been ecstatic with the news and had gone off about the possibilities of using my ability. Calrod had snarled and looked ready to charge across the room at her.

He wasn't the only one even more on edge now. Arkon had told Jasmine she was staying at Cyrene's house from now on. I'd waited for her to argue, but she'd given in. The attack at the shop was too much for her, too. She'd held it together while we were there, but I had no doubt she'd fallen apart the second she was alone with Arkon. They had so much more on the line, and I could tell she was furious with herself for not being able to fight back.

All that did was make me want to learn more about my abilities, so I could fight for us all just as hard as Calrod and his brothers were, as Morgan was doing.

Not that I'd said any of this to Calrod yet. I didn't have to think too hard to know how that conversation would go.

"So," I said while we continued to sit in the dark car, "it's later."

Calrod's hands twisted around the steering

wheel, his glowing blue eyes the only light. He grunted and climbed out. He stalked around the front of the vehicle and yanked open my door. Shit. Looked like the night wasn't even close to being over.

"Calrod," I started, but he growled. Rolling my eyes, I got out and made for the front door. "This isn't over."

The car door slammed behind me, and he stomped his way up the porch steps. The heat from his body pressed into my back. The slight crackle of fire in his hands sounded, along with his muttered curse. That'd been happening every few minutes since he'd shown up at the antique shop. I unlocked the front door and tossed my purse to the couch. Calrod followed, securely locking the door behind him.

"You should get some sleep," he said, turning his back to me and staring out the front windows.

"I'm not sleeping until we talk."

"Nothing to talk about. You heard Cyrene just as I did. No warding will keep Carridan from getting to us."

"And that means what?" I demanded.

"You know what," he shot back, still refusing to look at me. "Go to sleep, Cara."

"You can't boss me around in my own house." I

stomped into the kitchen, banging open cabinets and slamming the coffee pot down while I worked on brewing a fresh round.

Sleep. How'd he think I'd be able to sleep right now? I'd been attacked by witches instead of demons this time, but damn, that was twice in the last few days some asshole had tried to kill me. I told myself after I shot the witch that I was okay. And mostly, I was. I'd killed that bastard to save Jasmine and me, to save her baby. I might've told Calrod I was no stranger to death, but my hands shook all the same. It wasn't only my life hanging in the balance. It was Calrod's.

I saw that look in his eyes at the shop, saw the knowledge that whoever came after me, he'd rip them apart, with his bare hands if he had to. He wouldn't let anyone get to me, which meant he'd be throwing himself in between Carridan and me. I was worried about me, yeah, but I was more concerned about him. I wasn't the one who was mentally unstable at the moment.

Here he was waiting for me to have a complete breakdown over my life being put in danger again, which meant he ignored what he was clearly going through. No matter what he told me, he wasn't ready to accept what I was to him. His emotions were all over the place. That fire going off in his hands told me loud and clear how close he was to exploding with rage and fear and whatever else he kept trying to hide.

What if it'd been Calrod at the shop today and not Arkon? What if those witches had overpowered him? An image of him lying dead on the ground, his eyes wide and staring, made my hands shake even worse.

"Damn it," I snapped, spilling grounds all over the floor.

Calrod hurried into the kitchen, pausing on the threshold. "Don't think you need coffee right now."

"No, you don't get to lecture me," I muttered, scooping up the grounds with the small dustpan I kept under the sink. "You don't get to do anything until you accept this." I waved my hand between us and waited.

"I did."

"No, you admitted that it was true, but you're not even close to accepting it. If you were, you wouldn't be keeping yourself on the other side of the fucking room from me." My face grew hot, and I was still trembling, but not from only fear anymore. "I know what you're doing, and you're going to stop."

"I'm not doing a damn thing except trying to keep you alive."

"By pushing me away."

His jaw clenched, and the sparks at his fingertips ignited into fully formed flames. "You don't understand."

"I've been attacked twice. I think I understand."

"No, you don't," he yelled, then ran his fiery hands through his hair, pacing into the living room, then right back to me. Those heated hands snagged my upper arms and dragged me into his chest. He bared his elongated fangs at me, and a throaty growl erupted from his mouth. I knew what he was doing and didn't flinch away, didn't even blink. "Carridan is one of the most ruthless princes in the Underworld. Do you have any idea what he'll do if he finds out what you mean to me?"

"I'm not running."

"You should," he snapped. "I can't watch you go through that torture, that pain because of me. This can't happen. It can never happen, not while he's alive."

"Then we kill him," I said simply, and he scoffed, letting me go. "What?"

"If Carridan shows up to Oak Hollow, he won't be alone." He backed away further. The second the resolve appeared in his eyes, my heart started to crack. "He'll bring every murderous wretch under his command and I," he hesitated, taking one more step, "I won't watch you suffer because of me. I fucked up once so many years ago. My family paid the price for it. The same can't happen to you."

The secret he'd been keeping from me, this was it. I started to ask him about it, but cut off my own question. One issue at a time. Whatever he thought he was guilty of, I doubted it was true, at least not in the way he believed. If he'd messed up that badly, Arkon and Dagon wouldn't have stayed by his side all these years. They loved and watched out for their older brother. They worried about him not having the life he should, the life they now had because of him keeping them safe over the years. I'd heard the stories from Arkon and Dagon, from Jasmine and Morgan. Calrod was the family's protector no matter what he appeared to think of himself.

I couldn't be the one to make him see that, though. They'd have to do it. But I could make him see that being with me wasn't going to condemn either of us. It'd save us. It'd save him.

"I never should've found you," he whispered. The pain in those few words made the crack in my heart widen a hint more. "I don't deserve this, or you. I'll just destroy whatever we might have together. It's what I do."

"So you're going to go through life pretending I don't exist?"

The hopeless look he gave me was the most vulnerable I'd seen from him yet, and I ached to go to him, to soothe away those frown lines etched in his brow. "It'd be better."

"That's bullshit," I exclaimed. "You say you don't want to see me in pain, but what you're saying now? What you're planning on doing? That hurts, Calrod. It'll always hurt. I can't just get over you, not when I know what you are to me. What we can have."

"The bond hasn't been sealed," he replied quietly.

"And that means what?"

"We haven't officially mated," he explained, and my cheeks burned, realizing how we'd do that. "It means if I leave you now, you'll have a chance to move on and get over me. It'll take time, but it's possible." His eyes flicked to the front door, and panic set in. I ran to it, throwing myself between him and it.

"And you?" I asked on a breath. "Will you ever get over me?"

"It's what I deserve."

"Going through life knowing I'm right here in this town, possibly with someone else? That's what you deserve? To be unhappy forever? Calrod," I whispered, reaching for his hand, but he stepped out of reach. "That's not living. That's, shit, I don't know what it is, but I won't let you do this."

"I'm not giving you a choice. I'm sorry. I'll keep watch from outside. You won't have to see me again." He turned and walked to the kitchen, probably heading for the garage door. I ran after him, barely cutting him off. "Cara, stop."

"No. I won't let you do this to yourself."

He moved back to the front door, but I snagged his arm, darted around in front, and shoved him as hard as I could. He didn't move, but he stopped. "You have to let me go."

"Why did you save me the other day?" I yelled. "Why, huh?"

"Don't do this."

"I want to know why if your plan was just to up and leave me. Why did you talk to me all these months? Come over to my house when you knew I was playing a game with you? You played back, Calrod. You came over, and you talked to me, you laughed with me," I rambled on, desperate to make him understand why he couldn't simply walk out that door. "You became a part of my life."

"I didn't mean to," he whispered roughly.

"Yes, you did. You're breaking my heart right now. Is that what you want, huh? Is it?" I shouted and pushed him again. "Why did you do it? You're not a bad person, so why?" I asked it over and over until finally, he snatched my wrists.

"Because you're mine," he yelled.

Fire erupted around our feet, but I wasn't afraid of it. Its heat cocooned me as if Calrod had his arms wrapped around my body. They reached out, caressing my legs and arms until I shivered with unbridled need.

"I'll always be yours," I whispered, and Calrod's eyes darkened. "You going to walk out that door, or are you going to make it official?"

For the length of a heartbeat, I thought I was going to lose him.

Then he wound his arm around my waist, lifted me onto my toes, and kissed me with the full weight of his desire behind it. His lips burned with delicious heat, and his tongue quickly stoked a fire burning deep inside my soul. The flames twisted around us while we maneuvered down the hall toward the bedroom.

"You're mine," he whispered against my lips. "And I willingly give you my heart."

I fisted my hands in his shirt, capturing his mouth in answer. At the doorway to my room, I let him go and stepped inside, shedding my shirt in the process. Calrod's hungry growl had me hot with anticipation of what was to come. I beckoned him forward and watched as my demon stalked closer.

7

Cara

Calrod prowled toward me in all his demon glory. His eyes raked over my torso, fixating on my rapidly rising and falling chest. With a wicked grin, he snapped his fingers, and my bra sparked, then turned to ash, burning off my body. I had a second to contemplate the possibilities of what else his fire could do, then he was before me.

His kiss was demanding, but so was mine. I tugged at his shirt, needing it off him. Needing to see and touch as much bare skin as possible. His shirt gone, I admired the light dusting of black hair across his chest and lower. My fingers followed the trail to the button on his dark denim. I popped it free, grinning up at him while I did. He cupped my cheek, running his thumb over my bottom lip. I sucked it into my mouth and pressed my hand flat to the bulge beneath his pants. He groaned, his hips shifting forward so he could push himself harder into my hand. Feeling him and how big he was, knowing what would fill me soon enough, set my desires off even more.

I dragged his head down, feverishly kissing him. It'd taken too damn long to get to this moment. Now that we were, I couldn't hold back how much I wanted him, all of him.

Just as I was ready to undo his jeans and have my way with him, his lips slipped from mine to my neck, then lower. I cursed, seeing stars while he sucked a perky nipple into his mouth. His other hand squeezed my ass, capturing me against his burning chest. Flames ribboned out from his hand, cupping my other breast. They rippled across my skin, then focused on my other nipple. My head fell back on a gasp at the pleasure shooting down my body. My hands needed to grab hold of something. They slid through Calrod's hair and gripped his horns.

His fangs grazed my skin, and the flames grew even hotter, but they never burned me. I loved every second of it. His mouth left my nipple, and his tongue plunged into my mouth while he worked at my jeans. They were gone fast enough, along with my boy shorts. I waited for him to touch me where I so desperately wanted. Instead, his lips curled into a mischievous grin. The flames that had been teasing my chest slithered their way down my body. The second they flowed between my legs, I let out a ragged moan, my back arching against Calrod's arm.

He kissed my neck and shoulders while those flames continued to massage my sex. I squirmed in his arms, needing more of him, but the pleasure was too much. Calrod sank to his knees, and keeping me upright with his arm, he spread my legs wider and sought out my bead with his tongue. The fire moved, rising up my body in undulating waves.

Somewhere amid the firestorm of ecstasy taking hold of me, I realized those flames, what I felt from them, was Calrod. What he felt, what he wanted, it was all laid bare in those flickering blue and white ribbons winding so lovingly around me. Caressing and loving while not giving me an ounce of pain.

His fingers plunged into my sheath. The bubble of pleasure that had been waiting to burst did so then. I cried out, unable to see straight while his tongue massaged my bead and his fingers took me without mercy. My inner muscles clenched, not wanting to let him go. With the last tendrils of the orgasm rippling through me, his hand slipped free, and he eased me onto the bed, covering me with his body.

I worked at his jeans, fighting to get his cock free so I could hold it in my hand. His warm chuckle made the fire flow freer around us, somehow not singeing the sheets or setting the wall alight. He shed the last of his clothes, and I closed my palms around his shaft. He was larger than I'd imagined, and a thrill shot through me. His reaction was immediate. His hips thrust forward, gently fucking my hands while his trailed everywhere along my naked skin. We rolled in the sheets, kicking the blankets to the floor without a care. I was utterly consumed by Calrod between his hands and his fire and never wanted to be anywhere else.

I pinned him to the bed, and his claws lightly grazed my sides. I shivered, then slithered down his body. My name was on his lips, but I closed my mouth around the soft tip of his cock and sucked hard. I worked my hands along his length, taking more of him in each time. While I licked him from base to tip, my gaze latched onto his hooded one. His lip twitched, and I wondered what he was up to. A burst of heat bloomed between my legs, and I shuddered, overwhelmed by a torrent of pleasure I wasn't ready for.

"That's not fair," I argued, gasping at a second surge of heat that had me dragging my nails down his thighs. "Calrod."

I ended up on my back, staring up into those shimmering blue eyes. He captured my wrists and placed my hands over my head. Languidly, he kissed his way from my lips to my neck, then lower, teasing my nipples into hardened points all over again. The sensation of his hardened shaft pressed against my thigh, so close to being buried inside me, left me anxious. I raised my hips, wanting him, but his chuckle said that wasn't about to happen yet.

The flames that had been dancing around us both moved lower until they rested between our hips. The fire condensed then morphed before slipping between my legs. Heat had my thighs falling open, then the fire was inside me, filling me as if Calrod thrust between my legs instead. My lips parted on a sigh that quickly turned into a moan. My back arched while Calrod used his fire to stretch my sheath again and again. On the cusp of my coming apart, Calrod grabbed hold of my hip with one hand and plunged inside.

I urged him on, digging my heel into his ass while I wrapped my legs around his waist. Even still, I sensed he held back, probably worried he'd hurt me. He wasn't small by any means. The slight tremble to his shoulders was all I needed to know he hesitated.

"You won't ever hurt me," I whispered. "Calrod, I want you, all of you."

His arms shook with how hard he struggled to maintain control. I sensed the strength in the corded muscles of his body and his worry about letting me experience all of him. But I wasn't concerned. I bucked my hips, nodding for him to let go and take me with everything he had. His hold on my hip tightened, then he withdrew and thrust his hips all the way forward.

Ecstasy exploded, and it was all I could do to hold on while he picked up the pace, claiming me as he needed to do. I saw it in his eyes, that primal instinct to mark what was his. I recognized that look because I was doing the exact same to him. His groan quickly joined the harsh sounds slipping from my lips. Every drag in and out of his body against mine only set me on fire more. The added sensation of his fire continuing to plunge inside me each time

Calrod moved sent me over the edge. He filled me so completely, and I only wanted more.

His hand slipped between our bodies, and he rubbed my clit. I squeezed my breasts, pinching my nipples while his hungry growl vibrated through us. My cries cut off, and I lost myself in the pleasure he gave me that no one else ever could or would. When he slipped free, I immediately wanted him back. He pulled me upright and onto his lap, burying his hands in my hair while I straddled his lap and let my tongue dance with his. I'd never get enough of this demon that was mine. He crushed me to him, his cock hardening against my sex. I adjusted my body, and he easily slid inside. Keeping a firm hold of my hips, he thrust upward while his mouth sought out my chest once again. Fire wound around and between us, lighting up the darkened room with the blue flames of his want.

We came apart a second time, clutching each other close. He buried his face in my neck, grunting with his release burning with fire inside me. I held him snug within my sheath, riding out the storm until we fell to the bed in a panting mess.

He smoothed my hair from my forehead, then pressed his lips there. His brow furrowed, and he opened his mouth, probably to ask if I was alright. I quickly cut off his question with a kiss, hugging him to me.

"I didn't know you could use your fire like that," I mused.

He relaxed and finally slipped his shaft from my body. I sucked in a sharp breath from another bout of pleasure filling me. "Neither did I, not until you."

When I first asked about his fire, he'd told me that it only hurt those he wanted it to. I hadn't been concerned it'd burn me, but damn, if I'd known what else he could use it for, I might've dragged him to my bed a lot sooner. I grinned, not planning on sleeping at all tonight. But glancing up at his face, all my musings vanished.

"What is it?" I asked, not liking the intensity of the growing shadow in his eyes.

"There's no going back now," he murmured.

"No regrets here," I promised.

"Cara," he started, but I rolled us over and straddled his body.

"You claimed me," I whispered, kissing him sweetly while I reached for his already swelling shaft. "Now it's my turn."

His tip teased my sex, then he was filling me one slow inch at a time. I sighed once our bodies were flush. His cock twitched inside me, and I used my inner muscles to squeeze him right back. His hands eased up my stomach, then cupped my breasts lovingly in his palms. Flames coated his skin, and my head fell back while I took my time riding him to that moment of pure bliss. I leaned back, resting my hands on his thighs and moving my hips. Fire pooled around my bead, then massaged it leaving his hands free to glide over the rest of me.

"Cara," he rasped, his hips bucking. "Look at me."

I adjusted my body and looked deeply into those dark blue eyes. I kept on staring, not blinking while we shuddered from the ecstasy pumping through our systems. Another layer of his tough exterior fell away before me. In those few seconds, I could have sworn I saw not only Calrod's heart but his soul, too. He was right. There was no going back, and I never wanted to.

I fell to his chest, desperate for his kiss. He wound his arms around me, rolled us over, and his fire surrounded us.

"You're doing it again," I said, then popped a blueberry into my mouth.

Calrod's lips stretched into a lazy grin I was falling in love with more and more every time I saw it. I could get used to seeing him smile this much. "Can you blame me?"

We'd been talking about random shit that didn't matter. He'd be in the middle of a sentence, and his eyes would wander across my naked body. He'd simply stare. Not that I could blame him. I was doing the same thing to him. He was on his side, lying across the foot of the bed. I'd scrounged up the last of the fruit I had in my fridge and a bottle of whiskey from the kitchen and brought it back to bed. Neither of us had seemed ready to go to sleep. Absently, I picked up another berry, smiling while I held it to my lips.

"What's that look for?" Calrod asked.

"What look?"

"That smile that says you're clearly thinking about more than that damn blueberry in your hand."

"It'd be nice if we could stay in this moment, you know?"

I lowered my hand without eating the berry. My chest grew tight, and for the first time in hours, I was cold. Or I was until a ribbon of fire stretched across the bed and quickly wound up my torso. I tried to smile, but it wouldn't come. Tears burned in my eyes, and I turned away to swipe at them, not wanting Calrod to see.

The bed shifted, and his arms slipped around my sides. He pulled me back into his embrace, holding me. I pressed the heel of my hand into my eye to stop the tears from falling. I had no idea why I was even upset. I was supposed to be thrilled right now, or at least I should've been.

"I'm fine," I heard myself say.

"Really? You sure about that?" he replied softly and pressed his lips to my shoulder.

"Yep. I am. Swear it. I mean, I should be, right? You and I are officially a thing now, and I'm happy about that, beyond happy, and I've never felt this alive. So yep, I'm perfect. Nothing wrong at all."

The snuggling bear of a man I'd fallen asleep with last night came out once again. He bundled me into his arms, drew me onto his lap, and hugged me. He lay us down on the bed and snagged one of the blankets from the floor to pull over top us, blocking out the lamplight. I kept whispering that I was fine but eventually gave up and let the emotions flow. Calrod's hold on me never lessened.

"I think the last few days finally caught up with you," he whispered after a while.

"I don't usually blubber like this."

His laughter was warm, and he kissed my cheek so sweetly, it brought tears to my eyes all over again. "I know what you're going through, I think. Least part of it. I might not be crying right now, but there's a lot going on in here." He placed his hand to his heart, his eyes shimmering beneath the blanket while he held my gaze. "I don't know how this is going to work or if I'm going to be any good at it, but I'm not letting you go, not for anything."

"I know. Same goes for me, with you, though."

He found my hand and brought it to his lips. His eyes darkened until the blue was almost black. A discontented growl rumbled through his chest. Before he even opened his mouth to speak, I knew I wasn't going to like what came out. "If I ask you to do something, will you swear to do it?"

"If you're about to ask me to go stay at Cyrene's place, the answer is no."

"Cara," he started, but I cut him off with a kiss.

"I get why Arkon wants Jas there, but I'm not pregnant, and I promised her I'd look after the shop. We can't just completely stop living until this threat is over," I argued. "Dagon's vision was summer. What if it's next summer, or the summer after that? I'm not going under house arrest while you parade around town hunting down more demons and witches and whatever else Carridan decides to send here."

"I'm a little harder to kill."

"And I'm not just some weak little human, remember?" I threw the blanket off us and climbed out of bed. "You heard Cyrene. There's more to what I can do than just speaking to the dead and seeing them."

"Like being possessed by them?" he muttered darkly. "You know how risky that is?"

"I do, but if there's a way I can use it to help, then I'm going to."

He was out of the bed and in front of me in seconds. "The hell you are. You just found all of this out. It'll take months, years even before you're ready to do anything to that magnitude."

"I'm a fast learner."

Sparks ignited his fingertips, and the temperature in the room rose a few degrees. "This fight is mine, not yours."

I poked him in the chest. "It became mine the second you walked into my life, stud."

"This isn't a damn game."

"I know it's not, but I'm not going to sit back and wave at you from a distance with a damn handkerchief in my hand, praying you come back to me.

You're not the only badass in this town who knows how to fight."

"They're demons and witches," he said, sounding at the end of his patience.

"And? If I recall, I helped you take out the first two, and I blew holes in one of the witches."

He cursed, running a hand down his face and turning his back to me. "Arkon and Dagon were right. Gods, this is impossible."

"What is?"

The look he shot me over his shoulder sent a burst of heat down my spine. "Loving a woman who's filled with enough fight, it's like there's a storm raging inside her. A storm that'll stand against anything in its way and challenge it to a fight to the death."

"I'll take that as a compliment."

"You're going to be the death of me," he growled, and I was in his arms a second later.

He picked me up and pressed my back into the wall while my legs wrapped tightly about his waist. His kiss was ravenous, taking everything I had to offer and then some. His hardened shaft pierced my sex, and I cried out against his lips, shuddering from the spike of pleasure he brought me. I didn't have to look to know his fire had joined us. Its heat caressed my body while his hands held me upright. He moved away from the wall, keeping himself buried inside me, and lay me out on the bed.

"You are a storm," he rasped, lightly tracing his claws up my body, between my breasts, and lovingly cupped my throat. His thumb trailed over my bottom lip, and his hips slowed to a stop. "A storm that isn't allowed to die on me. I can't lose you, Cara."

"Right back at you," I breathed, holding his hand. "Calrod."

He withdrew his shaft all the way, and I shivered from the loss of his heat. It wasn't for long. He climbed onto the bed the rest of the way, his kisses and touch turning frantic. When he buried himself inside me again, I saw the unspoken promise in his eyes. I gave the same one right back, praying we'd both get to keep them.

If Carridan dared to show his face in Oak Hollow, I'd do whatever I could to see him dead before he took Calrod from me. Somehow, I had to find a way to speak to Cyrene and get her to start teaching me just what I was truly capable of. If it came down to a fight, Calrod wasn't going to stand alone. I'd waited too damn long to have him by my side.

No one was stealing him from me, not while the storm still raged inside me.

"CALROD, if you aren't going to stop that growling, you can leave," Cyrene ordered.

I grinned at Calrod who was standing near the door of the library. The annoyed look on his face had only worsened since this morning when I'd told him I wanted to speak with Cyrene. He'd pressed me as to why and I'd finally blurted my reasoning. That had led to an argument that somehow ended up with the two of us naked and having sex on the couch. The angry quickie had left me reeling in more ways than one.

But Calrod had given in and brought me to Cyrene's house.

From the regret burning in his eyes, he wished he hadn't.

"Come on," Jasmine said, appearing at Calrod's side. She took hold of his arm and gave him a tug. "You can keep me company in the saloon. Bored out of my mind today." She winked at me and dragged Calrod away.

I was in for it later, I could feel it. Guessed it

wouldn't be so terrible if every argument we had led to sex.

"Now," Cyrene said, clapping her hands. "Time to understand what your gift is."

"Aside from seeing the dead?" I glanced around the library. All the bookshelves were gone today, as was the massive cauldron that had taken up space in the center of the room. For the first time, I noticed the white outline of a massive circle on the floor. Connected it to it were three more, as well as some other symbols I didn't recognize. "What's this?"

"A way to help channel the magic flowing through your veins. Many humans are born with magic, but very few manage to manifest it. You, Morgan, and Jasmine are extremely unique."

"There's a lot of mediums, aren't there?"

Cyrene held up her finger. "Yes, but you're not a medium, not in that sense." She motioned me to stand in the center of the circle. "Have a seat and get comfortable."

I did as she said while she pressed her hand to the largest circle. It gave off a faint, white glow and the air crackled around me. "Now what?"

"Close your eyes and tell me what you feel."

"Just like that?" I asked.

Cyrene nodded. "Magic isn't always complicated."

Trusting she knew what she was talking about, seeing as she was a witch and I was extremely new to magic, I shut my eyes and waited. The floor was hard under my butt, and I shifted around, trying to get comfortable. My hands rested on my knees, and I sat there, listening to my breathing, wondering what was supposed to happen.

"I don't feel anything," I murmured after what felt like a while.

"You're listening, not feeling," Cyrene pointed out. "Take a deep breath, let it out, and simply feel what's around you."

I frowned but shifted again and worked at feeling. I focused on the air against my skin. It was warm, but not Calrod warm. There was almost a weight to it, and I tilted my head, wondering from what. My body swayed slightly as if being buffeted by a current of water. A light touch brushed against my cheek. Unlike when a spirit did it, there was no cold. Instead, it left a tingling sensation. The more I concentrated on it, the more it intensified until my fingers were tingling, too. A pressure built in my gut, then my hands jerked. My eyes flew open in time to see a burst of violet light explode out of my fingertips, striking the wall with a loud crack.

I jumped to my feet the same time Calrod came running. "What was that?" I asked, staring at my hands then Cyrene, who was smiling. "I did that?"

"Yes and no," she said.

Calrod growled, entering the room and coming right for me. He took my hands and looked me over. "What are you showing her?" he demanded.

"That spirits aren't the only thing she can be possessed by."

"What?" we asked together.

"What's happening?" Jasmine asked, joining us. "What did I miss?"

"I'm not sure," I said, shaking my head. "I don't understand. How can I be possessed by something other than a spirit?"

"Our world is filled with energy, something Morgan would be more than happy to tell you about," Cyrene explained, slowly strolling around the circle, her violet skirts trailing on the floor behind her. "Spirits are, after all, just another form of that energy moved on to a different plane than our own."

"Okay," I said slowly, still unsure where she was going with this.

"Magic too is merely energy being manipulated," she went on. "And as such, it leaves behind residue, an essence. It leaves behind a ghost of itself. Acts of nature do the same. There's nothing quite like the power of a thunderstorm."

I gulped, and Calrod's hold on my hands tightened. "What I did just now, that was me tapping into the spirit of your magic?"

"Yes, and that is merely the beginning." Cyrene approached, her violet gaze searching. "In all my years on this earth, I've seen magic begin to wane, seen it fade away. But then the fates brought me to you and Jasmine and Morgan. You three are just the beginning of magic finding its way back. Without it, I fear of what's to come."

"Why do you make it sound like you're not only worried about Carridan?" Calrod asked quietly. "Cyrene, what else have you seen?"

"Far too much," she whispered. "But there's time for that later. There'll be time." She glanced sadly toward the library doorway as if looking for someone. The heartbreak in that gaze made my own chest ache. She shook her head, and it was gone. "Night's not over. Back to the circle, Cara. And Calrod, why not show us a bit of fire? Let's see what else she can tap into."

"No." Calrod's growl was deep and rumbled through his body and right into me.

"Do you want her defenseless?" Cyrene argued.

"Fire is dangerous. It has a mind of its own if you don't know what you're doing," he snapped.

"One way or another, she'll learn. You can be at her side helping, or you can leave. You choose."

The blue aura around his body pulsed, and his hands warmed. Not looking at me, he broke from my touch and stalked to the far side of the room. Dark blue flames grew in his upright palms, stretching higher and higher with each deep breath he sucked in and let out through his nose. When his gaze finally connected with mine, it had me wondering if I was making the right choice. I might think I was ready to learn, but I was pushing Calrod too hard, too fast. He'd barely accepted that I was his mate. Now, I was learning how to fight right in front of him. I started to apologize, but he growled, lifting his lip and exposing his fangs.

"If you want to learn to fight," he snapped, "then you best pay attention."

He unleashed a torrent of fire to soar around the room. The flames took shape, morphing into a phoenix that called out as it flew higher and higher then came right for me. It hovered, wings flapping and sending embers tumbling to the floor around my feet.

It wasn't the phoenix staring back at me from those white eyes, though. That was all Calrod. The phoenix cried out one more time, then burst into one bright blue flame. His hands were clenched at his sides, black smoke trailing from between his fingers.

CALROD THREW the front door open to my cottage and stepped aside so I could enter. He'd been fuming since we'd left Cyrene's. I'd never seen his eyes so full of fire before or felt such heat coming off him.

"I'm okay," I assured him, holding my right hand to my chest. "Just a little burn."

He slammed the door shut but didn't turn to face me yet.

"I'm sorry," I said for the twentieth time at least. "I thought since the fire was yours, it wouldn't hurt me. It was my fault I got burned, but it's not that bad. See?" I held up my right hand where the fire had scorched my skin. "Cyrene's salve's already got it mostly healed. It won't even scar."

Smoke drifted out of Calrod's fists, and when he finally glanced over his shoulder at me, more flowed out of his nose. Shit. I was in trouble. A whole heaping lot of trouble.

"Calrod," I tried, but his snarl cut through my words, and he whipped around.

"I told you fire is dangerous, but you didn't listen. Neither did Cyrene. You're not ready to be messing with this level of magic," he ranted. "Not even close."

"I can do it, though. You saw me."

"I saw you get burned," he yelled, then threw his head back with a curse. "That wasn't my fire, not anymore. I couldn't control it, and neither could you. Fire feels what you feel. If you're intimidated by it, scared, it'll know, and it'll take over." His gaze shifted to my right hand, and he spat out several words in demonic.

"Don't do that shit," I said. "What did you say?"

He worked his jaw back and forth, then muttered, "I said you're a fool, and I can't do this."

"We're back to that? Really? One accident, and you no longer think you can handle being with me?"

"That's not what I said, damn it." He came to me, holding my right wrist in his grip. "Do you have any idea what it's like watching you use these powers knowing that any day now, you might try to use them against another demon? Or gods forbid, Carridan himself?" He let me go, stomping around the living room while he scratched at the scruff on his face. "You can't lie to me and say you don't plan on being right by my side in case he shows up."

I screwed my lips to the side. He was right. I wasn't going to lie, so I said nothing.

He scoffed. "You're messing with shit that's too damn dangerous for you. You don't understand what he's capable of, but I do. I've seen it, and you, you're acting like it's just another day."

"I'm not about to let you fight him alone. Morgan's learning, too, so she can fight, and we both know if Jasmine wasn't pregnant, she'd be doing the same thing." I marched to him, snagging his arm to pull him to a stop. "You said you can't lose me, but I can't lose you either, Calrod. I won't, so if this is what it takes to make sure that doesn't happen, then I'm doing it, damn the consequences. You want to be pissed off about it, then fine. But don't you dare ask me not to fight for you."

"I won't watch him kill you," he said, his voice ragged.

"Then let me help you kill him instead."

"Nothing but a fucking storm," he grumbled, then he had me in his arms, his lips slanted over mine. "One that's going to consume us both." His fire snaked around us, pushing me hard into his chest.

His desperation seeped right into me, and I tugged at his shirt. Clothes, we were wearing too many damn clothes. His t-shirt disappeared, and mine quickly followed, my bra, too. I reached for his jeans, but he spun me around. Shoving aside my hair, he nuzzled my neck while his hand slipped down my body, undid my pants, and pushed inside my boy shorts. He wasted no time in thrusting his fingers into me. I cursed, digging my nails into his arm and fumbling to have his mouth again. With an annoyed grunt, he shoved my jeans further down my hips, then his hand returned to driving me crazy. My hips bucked, riding out the quickly building pleasure inside me.

When I was right on that edge, ready to topple over, his hand withdrew, and he turned me back around, lifted me into his arms, and made his way to the couch. He set me on my feet long enough to relieve me of my pants while I quickly undid his enough to find his pulsing cock, ready and waiting. He sank onto the couch, drew me onto his lap, and brought me down over his shaft. I bit my lip, winding my arms around his neck while he held onto my hips, holding me steady while he drove into me again and again.

His claws lightly pricked my ass, and I reached for his horns, squeezing them tight. Whatever sliver of control he'd had left vanished. Blue flames burst to life around us, blocking the living room from sight. I rode him hard, needing to feel as much of him as I could. He growled my name, and I looked into his eyes while we came apart. His brow furrowed, and I cried out, my body shuddering in his arms. His release burned within me, and I slumped forward. A fine sheen of sweat slicked our skin. He kissed his way down my neck to my shoulder, then gently lifted my chin.

"No being reckless," he whispered. "If this comes to a fight, you will not rush in blindly even if it means saving me. Promise me that much."

"I can't," I replied sadly. "Storms are reckless and unpredictable. That never changes."

I expected him to get mad all over again and set me aside. Instead, he picked me up, cradling me in his arms, and made his way down the hall to the bedroom. He set me on the bed, shed the rest of his clothes, and climbed on with me. We said nothing else the rest of the night, but it was far from quiet. That was the incredible bond I had with Calrod.

Neither of us needed to speak, but we knew exactly what the other was thinking, what they needed.

Right now, he needed every second he could get with me. Every touch and kiss, every moment to remind him Carridan hadn't come yet, and we were both still here. That I could give him, and I always would.

8
____

Calrod

The shop was finally empty of customers, and I took full advantage of it. I crept around tables and display shelves, flipped the closed sign in the window, and locked the front door. Once that was done, I let my glamour fall.

Cara wasn't paying attention, and I continued winding my way through the store until I was on the other side of the u-shaped counter. Cara had been running the shop for the last two weeks, and what a ride those weeks had been. She'd wanted me to accept that she was mine, and I had. There was no more holding back. No more keeping my emotions to myself, not when it came to her and what she did to me.

The intensity with which my inner fire burned for her was a constant inferno that could only be calmed by her touch. It wasn't only our bond that had me on fire, though. That woman tested my patience every damn day, wanting to learn how to use her ability more. Determined to figure out a way to keep me alive if it was the last thing she did.

There was no stopping her from learning more, but she held off on reaching for my fire, which I was grateful for. Not that it'd last. Or was my fire the most powerful force she could tap into. Cyrene had mentioned something about thunderstorms again. Cara's eyes had lit up while I'd inwardly cursed.

I hadn't been able to erase the image that had formed in my head after that. Cara not merely acting like a storm but becoming one. Was that even possible?

I shook my head with a quiet grunt. That was a worry for tomorrow. Now, I was going to take every day we had together as a gift and live it to the fullest. Cara was bringing me back to life and damned if I wasn't going to dive in headfirst just as she had. I raised my hand, and focusing on Cara, I brought a small burst of fire to life. It lazily slipped through the air and wrapped around her body. She sighed, her shoulders relaxing while the blue flames danced along her skin. Grinning, I directed them lower, and she gasped, her hands clutching the edge of the counter.

"Calrod," she rasped. "Someone might walk in."

"Not if the door's locked."

The sound of her rapid breathing had my jeans stretched taut over my groin. Unable to resist the pull of her presence, I walked around the counter, ramping up the heat of the fire. Her knees trembled, and she shuddered. A string of barely coherent curses fell from her lips.

"Not... fair," she muttered. Her forehead scrunched, and her eyes closed. Her cheeks reddening, she bit her bottom lip.

"You have the most beautiful face when you're coming," I whispered in her ear, and the quivering mess she'd become fell into me. I kissed her sweetly, trapping her body between me and the counter. "I could watch it all day long."

"Didn't you do that last night?" she mused with a grin. Her quiet moan quickly turned into a cry, and she shook from the force of her release.

"And I plan on it doing it every night."

She turned to look at me, and I kissed her, easing

my hands under her shirt to cup those sweet mounds. With a quick pinch of my fingers, I undid the hooks of her strapless bra and tossed it behind me. Her nipples hardened against my fire-coated palms, and her tongue teased my mouth. I shifted my hips forward, and she reached around, straining to reach the button on my jeans. I meant to prolong our afternoon tryst, but she overwhelmed my senses too much. I slid my hands down her body and shoved her pants and boy shorts out of the way. Quickly, I pulled myself free of my jeans, spread her legs with my foot, and she leaned against the counter. I adjusted her body and eased my cock between her thighs, rubbing along her dripping wet sex.

"Calrod," she moaned, pressing her hand over mine at her hip.

With a bit of guidance from my hand, I eased into her sheath, meaning to take it slow. But, as I was quickly learning, nothing with Cara was ever slow. Her inner muscles tensed, and she squeezed my hand, wanting more. I gave her exactly that, thrusting forward, so she took all of me. We cursed together, then I was moving, her heels leaving the floor with each buck of my hips. The blue flames coursed faster around our bodies, pulsing in time with my heartbeat. She jerked against me, her body clutching me hard while ecstasy visibly consumed her. I followed seconds later, burying myself deep inside her while my shaft pulsed.

"You're going to spoil me with all these damn quickies," she said with a teasing smile at me over her shoulder.

"I see nothing wrong with that."

I wrapped my arms around her, hugging her while I breathed in deeply and let it out. This was usually how our encounters turned out lately. The bond between us burned too hot to be dragged out for long. Worse if we'd been parted for a few hours. The days she was here, and I went with Dagon or Arkon to scout the town, I spent most of the time terrified she would be attacked. Then I'd see her, and we couldn't get to her cottage fast enough. Thank the gods her hatchback was roomy enough we didn't always have to.

What left me even more shaken most days was how much I'd fallen in love with simply being with Cara. She was in my arms when I went to sleep and beside me when I woke up. I hadn't been to my house hardly at all unless it was to snag fresh clothes. I hadn't even taken on any new jobs, not wanting to be away from her unless it was business involving Carridan. I was getting used to this life with her. The fear of losing that left me with nightmares most nights. I hugged her again, keeping her safe in my arms.

"What do you think about heading home early today?" I murmured, slipping free of her body.

She shivered, then shoved her ass into the cradle of my hips. "As much as I'd love to do that, I have a couple of crates to get through still. If you want to head out, though, I don't mind."

I grunted. "As if I'd leave you here alone."

"Not the first time."

"If you're staying, I'm staying." I handed her pants back to her, and we traipsed to the bathroom in the back to clean up.

"Did something happen you're not telling me about?" she asked once we'd opened the shop up for business again.

"Nope, why?"

"Calrod. Remember what I said about lying? And how you suck at it?"

I kept my face blank, but fire sparked at my fingertips. She crossed her arms, nodding to my smoking hands. "You'll think I'm paranoid."

"You're already ungodly overprotective. Paranoia doesn't surprise me at this point."

"It's really nothing."

"Uh-huh, then why did you go from being okay with me at the shop alone last week to not letting me out of your sight at all this week unless I'm with Cyrene?" she accused.

I rolled my eyes toward the ceiling, knowing what she would say the second I admitted what had me worried. "It's been quiet since the attack from the witches."

"Isn't that a good thing? Maybe the new warding Cyrene put around the town is working."

"It's too quiet," I growled, and Cara sighed. "Carridan knows we're here. Why's he waiting? Even if the warding is working, we'd still see signs of his demons trying to get in, or he'd be here himself."

"I'm not going to call you paranoid," she said, "but maybe we take these quiet days as a gift for now. We know he's coming, but every day that he's not here trying to kill you is another day we get to simply be together."

I cupped her cheek, my thumb brushing over her bottom lip. "You're right."

She grinned. "I know I am."

"Still think we should leave early."

She glanced at the clock on the wall between two paintings of the mountains and tilted her head.

"Give me another hour, then we can go. Happy?" She kissed my cheek and headed to the counter.

Brow arched, I sent a little burst of heat her way, and she cursed, her hazel eyes alight with desire all over again.

"Keep distracting me, and it'll be two hours."

"Two hours it is then," I whispered to myself, trying not to worry that the quiet of the last couple of weeks wasn't an omen for something even worse waiting to come to Oak Hollow.

"Why are we at my cottage for this?" Cara asked a couple of days later.

"Because here there are active spirits," Cyrene explained. "You haven't tried to tap into their energy yet, and I think it's time. Unless Calrod wants us to try fire again."

I growled, crossing my arms stiffly over my chest. "Not happening."

"Then spirit energy it is."

The three of us stood outside Cara's cottage, near the woods around the back. Cyrene had shown up in a whirlwind of leaves with an update that really wasn't much of one. There were no signs of Carridan or his demons heading for Oak Hollow. She hadn't even seen anything coming for us. It should've been good news, but the same paranoia I'd been fighting had been reflected back at me in Cyrene's glowing eyes. She didn't trust the silence either. And with each day that passed, Jasmine grew closer to having the baby. I talked to Arkon at least once a day, trying to keep him from losing his mind with worry. He'd yelled at Dagon a few times about getting a damn vision to let him know it'd be alright. Sadly, our youngest brother hadn't seen anything about any of us. Neither of us could blame Arkon for his freak-outs.

Dagon's lack of visions made me trust the peace and quiet even less.

"What am I supposed to do?" Cara asked, dragging me from playing out one terrible scenario after another.

"The same as you've done before. Feel the energy around you, tap into it, and use it."

"Use it how? It's spiritual energy. I don't even know what that is, not really."

"Trust yourself," Cyrene told her.

I bit back my retort on how that wasn't always good advice. The first time Cara attempted to use the ghost of my fire, she'd burned herself. Sometimes, you needed more than trust. I braced myself, ready to lunge forward if training went sideways today.

The overcast day seemed to darken the longer I watched Cara. She'd shut her eyes, but nothing seemed to be happening. I wondered if she wasn't able to pick up on the energy, then her face paled. When her lips turned blue, I ran forward, only to be stopped by Cyrene.

"Let her be," she whispered.

"She looks like she's dying," I snapped.

"Just give her a moment. Trust her."

I ground my teeth, tempted to toss Cyrene out of my path. Her glare said I'd be the one getting thrown across the yard. Cara gasped, and my gaze flicked back to her. She was even paler than before, and her eyes rolled back into her head. Her body collapsed to the ground. This time, I shoved my way past Cyrene.

"Cara?" I hauled her limp body into my arms. She was freezing. "Cara, talk to me, damn it."

A cool touch pressed against my neck. I turned. My fire went cold, and something inside me shattered. Hovering to my right was Cara. Her body shimmered, and her wide gaze shifted from her body in my arms to her see-through hands. She looked like she was talking, but there was no sound.

Time screeched to a halt. I reached for Cara, but she vanished. A furious snarl built with the inferno in my chest. I was ready to unleash hell on Cyrene, the witch who caused this to happen. But Cara's body shifted, and she sucked in a breath like she was coming up for air.

"Shit," she mumbled, trembling. "That, I never want to do again."

I cocooned her in my arms, holding her tight as I could. Relief washed through me, realizing she wasn't dead. She leaned back, and I held her face, studying every inch of her skin regaining its color. She started to speak, but I crushed my mouth to hers. She kissed me right back, clutching at my shoulders.

"Sorry," she whispered. "I'm sorry. I had no idea what I was doing."

"A part of you did."

At the sound of Cyrene's voice, I snarled, set Cara behind me, and planted myself between them. "Leave, now."

"This is part of her growing in her magic," Cyrene said, but I didn't want to hear it.

I'd just watched my mate collapse to the ground, dead, and then turn into a spirit. My claws grew, desperately wanting to bury themselves in Cyrene and rip her heart out. She glared right back at me, then her eyes shifted to Cara. Her face softened, and she blinked as if coming out of a daze. She shook her head and backed off.

"I'll give you time to recover," Cyrene murmured. "I'm sorry for pushing you, Cara."

"It's fine," she said, but I growled over her words. It was not fine, not even close.

Cyrene's brow crinkled, and she looked like she wanted to say more to me. Then, she brought her arm up, bringing the leaves and wind with it. They swirled around her. By the time the last one fell, Cyrene was gone.

"Calrod." Cara slipped her hand into mine, but I couldn't get my claws to retract. Not wanting to accidentally hurt her, I tried to pull away. She came right back and planted herself in front of me. She held my cheek, then molded herself to my body. The sweet smell of a gentle rain surrounded me, soothing the fire that needed to unleash itself. I let out a shaky breath, then closed my arms around her in a protective cage. "I think we could use a drink," she murmured.

I nodded, unable to get the words out past the lump that had formed in my throat. I never wanted to see her like that again, pale and cold as death.

When we entered the kitchen, the house phone was already ringing. Cara was going to ignore it, but I said she should answer it. She gave me a look but hurried to grab the cordless off the table.

"Hello? Dagon, just stop for a second. I'm fine," she said in a rush. She nodded and sighed. "I know, but it's not what you think."

I held out my hand, and she told Dagon she was passing him over to me. "Dagon."

"What the hell happened?" he demanded. "Shit, I thought she was dead. I saw her dead and hovering over you. You guys need to get out of there right now."

Cara mimed she was going to get us some drinks. I gave her a brief smile, then retreated to the living room. "That already happened, but like she said, it's not what you think." I gave him the quickest explanation possible for what I'd witnessed Cara do outside. Reliving that moment wasn't something I intended to ever do again. "When did you have the vision?"

"Right before I called. This is bad."

"How?"

"I'm getting visions of things after they've already happened," he yelled, and I thought I heard Morgan in the background trying to calm him down. "I didn't want to say anything to Arkon, but I saw the fight at the shop with the witches a whole day after it happened. It's never been like that before. Close, but not late, not after an event."

I gripped the phone harder, leaning to peer into the kitchen. Cara had poured two glasses half full of whiskey but was sipping from the bottle. "You think something's interfering with your visions?"

"Makes sense. Might be why I'm not getting any and if I'm getting them too late to help?"

"Don't be so hard on yourself."

"How can I not be?" he yelled, frantic. "I was counting on my visions to give us more clues, and now they're useless."

"Take a breath and stop beating yourself up. We knew Carridan coming after us wouldn't be simple," I muttered. "Call Cyrene and see if there's something she can do to help. If not, I suggest we up the patrols around Oak Hollow and try to convince Morgan and Cara that staying here isn't worth it."

"Good luck with that one," he said with a growl. "I'm sorry."

"For what?"

"For what you must've gone through in those few seconds," he replied.

I gritted my teeth, grunting in response.

"I'll let you go so you can take care of yourself, too," Dagon said. "If anything changes, I'll let you know." He hung up, and I set the phone on the coffee table.

"Dagon done freaking out?" Cara asked after I returned to the kitchen.

I took the glass of whiskey she offered and drained it.

Her brow arched, and she hopped up on the counter, nursing her own glass. "That good, huh?"

"He's worried about his visions," I said, knowing lying was pointless. "The one he just had of us came too late to warn us. And he hasn't seen anything in weeks."

"Can someone mess with him like that?"

"It's not out of the realm of possibilities," I admitted. My gut twisted, knowing immediately who would be able to go to such lengths to mess with Dagon. She, like Arkon, was adept at using magic when it suited her. She was a born manipulator. I hadn't heard what happened to her once I fled the Underworld with my brothers. If she was involved, the truth I wasn't ready to come clean about yet was going to be out in the open whether I liked it or not. "Cyrene would be better suited to answer that question," I added, hoping to change the subject.

Cara's hand covered mine around my glass and dragged me to her. She took the tumbler from me and, using her legs, drew me into her warmth. "It's not her fault, what I did out there," she said quietly, misinterpreting my annoyed growl for continued anger at Cyrene. "You can't hold it against her for giving me a bit of a push to see what I can do. You want to be grumpy, you can be grumpy with me."

"Who said I wasn't?"

"Calrod," she started, but talking wasn't what I had in mind for the rest of the day, not after what I'd seen her do, seen her become right before my eyes.

Burying my hand in her hair, I brought her to me and kissed her. She squeezed me between her thighs, her quiet murmur of desire pulsing through my blood. My other hand slammed into the wall behind her while that horrifying moment replayed itself over in my mind. My claws burst free and dug into the plaster. We weren't nearly close enough. Hauling her into my arms, I carried her to the bedroom, kicking the door shut.

I JERKED AWAKE WITH A SNARL, reaching for the knife I kept under my pillow. Silver light filled the bedroom, and I relaxed. I wasn't in the Underworld. I wasn't being betrayed all over again. I was with Cara in her cottage. It'd been a couple of days since Dagon realized someone was magically handicapping his visions.

During that time, I'd been distracted, thinking about the one person I'd hoped to forget. Every night, I'd been tormented by her damn face sneering at me while my world crumbled.

This last dream had been the worst. She'd had Cara in her clutches. I hadn't been able to get to her in time. I turned, expecting to see a swath of black curly hair on the pillow beside me, but the bed was empty.

"Cara?" I climbed out of bed, snagging my jeans from the floor. "Cara? Damn it, woman."

Keeping the knife clutched in my hand, I crept out of the bedroom. The rest of the house was dark. Heart racing and the demon rage ready to take hold, I checked every single room, but she wasn't here. Furious, I snarled. A noise came from the garage, and I took off toward it. I swung open the door and let out a grunt of relief. Cara stood in front of the workbench, a pile of clay taking shape in front of her. She had on the crop top and short knit shorts she wore around the house.

"Hey, sorry if I woke you up," she said, not turning around. "Couldn't sleep."

I was still fighting the building fire inside me and didn't bother trying to answer.

"Calrod? Shit, what's with the knife?" she asked.

"Woke up, you weren't there," I muttered. "Sorry, I uh, didn't mean to scare you."

"You didn't. You okay?"

"Yeah, good."

She came toward me, and the details of my nightmare flashed before my eyes. Cara being held captive by a sword at her throat. The woman behind her cackled with delight. I'd stretched out my hand to save her but the sword sliced across her neck. Too late. I was too damn late.

"You're shaking," Cara whispered, taking a firm hold of my hand. "Calrod, look at me."

I tried to turn away, but she held my cheek and slowly moved my face toward hers. I told myself that this was real and not a nightmare. But when I glanced down, all I saw was blood. I blinked, and it was gone. The knife slipped from my fingers, clattering to the floor. Instinct took over. I lifted Cara off her feet, capturing her mouth at the same time. I carried her to the worktable and sat her on it, desperate to feel her and chase away the horrors sleep had brought me.

I yanked her shirt over her head, massaging her chest while my fire burned around us. She pressed her breasts into my hands, and I teased her nipples. Her breath quickened, and she snaked her hands between our bodies. She undid my jeans and slid her hands inside. I groaned at her holding me, squeezing me while she pumped down my shaft. Lifting her off the table with one arm, I tugged her shorts and panties off, tossed them over my shoulder, and lowered my lips to her thigh. I eased her legs apart wider, letting my fire lead the way. Her head fell back with a curse the second the flames condensed and filled her sheath.

I sought that sweet bundle, massaging it while her hips jerked. My fingers joined the flames, filling her sweet depths. She grabbed my horns, pressing my head closer, and I obliged, ravishing her with my tongue. She cursed, her legs falling open even more, and I couldn't stand it any longer. I shoved my jeans out of the way, kicked them aside, and eased my cock into her soaking wet sex.

She grabbed hold of my horns, and I growled, thrusting forward until our bodies met. I brought her closer to the edge of the table, squeezed her hips, and plunged home again and again. She lay over the table, cupping her breasts and pinching her nipples. The sight of her giving herself to the pleasure sent me over the edge. The blue flames reached the ceiling, churning around us and blocking out the rest of the world. The fire lovingly caressed Cara's skin, and she cried out a second time, her hips bucking wildly in my grip.

My body trembled with the release, but it wasn't nearly enough. Cara sat up, kissing me frantically as if she'd picked up on the anxiety still tearing me apart. She slipped off the table, shoved me onto the wood chair by the table, and sank onto my lap. Thankfully, the chair was already against the wall, or we would've tipped over.

The blue and white flames came with us, moving through the garage and burning so bright, they were nearly blinding. I ran my hands through her hair then down her back. She pressed herself as close as she could get, her sex rubbing along my quickly hardening shaft. When she pierced herself with me, we groaned. There was nothing else at that moment except Cara. Her scent surrounded me, and her soul reached out and touched mine. We'd had some intense bouts of sex before, but this one was different. She slowed, then stopped with me seated perfectly inside her. Our gazes locked, and time simply stopped. I took in every detail of her face then, how her eyes were so full of life and brimming with the love she had for me. The fine sheen of sweat on her forehead that glistened in the firelight. The energy that hummed within her body and burst into me. The flames compressed around us, then we couldn't move fast enough.

I kissed her while we shuddered together. I swallowed her cries, clutching her to me like the lifeline she'd become, dragging me out of the darkness. When we finally broke apart, she trailed her fingers down my cheek.

"You're going to have to tell me what that dream was about," she whispered.

I kissed her, hoping she'd leave it at that.

"Calrod," she said against my lips. "Talk to me. I know you've been keeping something from me. I'm going to guess your nightmare had something to do with it."

"Never said it was a nightmare."

"Didn't have to." She wrapped her arms around me, hugging me.

My fire slowly receded then faded out of sight with a final crackle. I glanced at the worktable and cursed.

"What?" Cara followed where I was looking and smirked. "Huh, that's fun."

"Think I ruined your project."

"Why would you say that? I think it looks perfect. Shit, I think you managed to fire everything I had in here," she said, laughing.

The piece she'd been working on that had barely taken form was now a twisting churning sculpture of what looked like flames. The heat had been hot enough to set the clay.

"Spill. What did you dream about?" she asked.

I growled, keeping her safe in my arms. "Doesn't matter."

"I think it does."

I stood, keeping her legs wrapped around my waist, and headed for the house. "Later," I assured her, not planning on telling her a damn thing. The last thing she needed to know was that I was having nightmares of her being killed by the woman who first betrayed me.

Besides, I wasn't Dagon.

It was merely a nightmare.

Not a sight I'd have to witness.

Again.

9

Calrod

Cara handed me a cup of coffee in a paper cup and a bag filled with pastries.

"What are these for?"

"For you to take a break," she said and spun me around.

We were in the shop, but I hadn't done much of anything since arriving except try not to pass out. Since the first nightmare I had of Cara dying, that was all I saw now when I closed my eyes. I hadn't done much sleeping the last few nights, too terrified to close my eyes and watch her die all over again. She knew about the dreams. Hard not to when I woke up clutching a dagger in one hand and snarling. Her touch was the only thing to ease me back to sleep, restless as it might be.

"I'm fine," I said, not budging though she kept nudging me to move.

"You're falling asleep standing up. Drink the coffee, eat a donut or two, and maybe take a nap."

"You want me to take a nap while you're here? Yeah, that's not happening."

"You're exhausted," she argued, cupping my face and pulling me down so our faces were level. She kissed one cheek after the other, then my lips. "If you won't sleep, then go sit down and relax, okay? I'll be fine for half an hour."

The bell above the door chimed, and I grunted. Cara gave me another quick kiss, then walked off to take care of the new customers. I hesitated at the threshold of the doorway leading to the backroom. I would've felt better if the spirits were still here. The oval painting with a ghost attached had been sold, and the spirits with the postcards had apparently gone. The shop was empty of ghosts.

"Twenty minutes," I muttered to myself. "Eat something, drain your coffee, and then you can go back out there."

I did just that, sinking onto the old couch back here.

I hadn't meant to let my eyes close, but they did. Images took shape, Cara at her cottage while she worked. I smiled, hoping the peaceful daydream would remain. The house vanished, and I stood outside in the middle of a road. Cara was too far away to reach, and standing behind her with a damn sword in her hand was Vanessa, the bitch who betrayed me. My flames whipped at her, but they never made contact. I sprinted, desperate to reach Cara, but the blade glided across her neck. Blood spilled down her front, and she toppled over. She was dead by the time I got to her—

I jerked awake on the couch, rubbing a hand down my face to chase away the remaining remnants of the nightmare. My coffee was gone, and I figured I'd make a pot back here to help keep me awake the rest of the day. I was about to start it, but Cara talking to someone gave me pause. She seemed to be discussing a painting on the wall. The second the other person responded, my demon rage exploded. I ran into the shop, sending a burst of fire ahead of me. The blue and white flames surrounded Cara, putting a wall between her and the woman she'd been speaking with.

"Calrod," Cara exclaimed, her eyes widening. "Your glamour."

"Don't need it," I snapped, dragging her behind me. "You fucking bitch."

The woman, who appeared like an ordinary human, pressed a hand to her chest, looking appalled. I bared my fangs, and her lips curled into a wicked grin. She laughed, and her glamour melted away, revealing the demon she was. She took a tentative step closer, but my fire reacted in kind, lashing out, ready to burn her alive. She shook out her mane of chestnut hair, her short ruddy horns poking through just behind her forehead. Her eyes flared a brilliant gold, and she raised a hand bearing claws toward Cara.

"Is that any way to greet me? It's been years, Calrod."

I pushed the fire closer, ready to kill her and be done with it, but the flames couldn't seem to get anywhere near her.

"You think I'd show up here and not have a safeguard against your fire?"

"Don't need fire to kill you," I warned.

"True, but ten demons are standing just outside the shop. You kill me, they charge in, and I know you're good, but will you be able to keep yourself and that woman alive?" She licked her lips, her eyes narrowing. She sniffed the air and snapped her jaws.

"So it's true. You traded in the love you had for me for such a lesser being. I'm disappointed in you."

"Oh, wait, I get it," Cara said, pushing past me before I could stop her. "You're the ex. Uh, you know, seeing you and hearing you talk in that god-awful voice of yours, it all makes sense now."

Vanessa, the demon I'd believed had loved me all those years ago, tensed. "Don't speak to me."

"Why? I'm sorry, do lesser beings intimidate you or something? Yeah, see, you're in my friend's shop, and you're threatening my mate, so how about you back off before I kill you."

I wrapped my hand around Cara's arm, but she waved me off as if this was a perfectly ordinary thing to be happening right then.

"You can't kill me," Vanessa snapped.

"Bet you I can. Want to find out?"

I growled, my grip tightening on Cara's arm. What game was she playing? She'd barely begun figuring out how to use her abilities. Even if she did manage to kill Vanessa, the demons she had waiting outside were more than enough to be a challenge. Besides, whatever magic Vanessa used to stand against my fire would most likely work against Cara's power.

"What do you want?" I demanded, wanting to get

her attention away from Cara.

Vanessa's eyes narrowed further, and her lip twitched like she was debating on throwing herself through the fire to get at my mate. "I've come with a message from Prince Carridan, of course. Give him what he wants, or he'll turn Oak Hollow into a graveyard."

"And what does he want?"

She laughed. "Aside from you and your brothers dead? I'm afraid you don't get to know. You never could see the big picture. None of you could. Especially not the prince and his princess."

I cursed her for speaking of my parents. "Carridan never should've come here."

"Why? You honestly believe you three can destroy him? Please. You should've let him kill you instead of running away. Now look at the mess you've caused. How much blood do the three of you want spilled before you hand over your lives?" She turned and sauntered toward the door. "Pity. She's a real looker, too. They all are. It'll be fun to mess up those faces of theirs before I kill them."

"You'll never get your hands on her." I shifted my body, blocking Cara from view.

Vanessa stopped at the door, the malicious intent in her gaze not giving me an answer. She opened the door and stepped out into the daylight. It slammed shut behind her. I ran after her, cursing that she'd been telling the truth about the extra demons. They piled into two SUVs and sped away, spraying gravel.

I locked the door and flipped the sign to closed. Every inch of me shook, and the constant rumbling in my chest drowned out all other sounds.

A hand fell on my shoulder, and I snarled, whirling around.

Cara didn't flinch in the face of my anger. "She seems terrible."

"I'm sorry," I whispered, then wildly shook my head. "What were you thinking?"

"I was protecting you like I said I would," she argued.

"You can't just challenge a demon like her to a fight. Gods, Cara, have you lost your mind? Do you have any idea what she would've done to you?"

I grabbed her by the arms, needing her to understand, but she couldn't because I hadn't told her the truth yet. I released her and stormed around the shop, leaving a trail of fire in my wake. Nothing I did made the flames go out. Vanessa had been here. She'd threatened Cara in person. What if my nightmare came true?

Cara walked into my path, and I growled. Her

brow arched, and she snagged my hand, also coated in flames. "Come on. We're going home before you set this place on fire. Then we're going to have a chat."

I was in no position to speak and let her pull me out of the shop, shove me into her car, and drive home. By the time we reached the cottage, my rage peaked, and I needed to destroy something. Anything. I walked straight through the house, then out the back door and into the yard. The first tree I came across, I unleashed my fury on. The trees didn't stand a chance. I scorched three of them, roaring to the forest while I lost control. What would've happened if I walked out of that backroom a few minutes later? Vanessa could've killed Cara the second she came into the store. I couldn't let my guard down for a second, not anymore.

Vanessa had already stolen so much from me. I would not let her take Cara, too.

Guilt slammed into me, and the flames gave out. I sank to my knees in the grass, digging my hands into the dirt. Cara ran around and knelt in front of me, hugging me to her. She ran her fingers through my hair, telling me it was fine. But it wasn't. It never could be.

"It's my fault," I blurted, falling back to sit on the

ground.

"What is?"

I angrily picked at the blades of grass, unsure how to even tell her the truth. She picked up my hand and squeezed it between hers.

"I'm right here. Whatever you did, it can't be as bad as you think."

"But it is. Everything that's happened, Carridan coming after my family, it's because of me."

I couldn't even look at Cara once the words started tumbling out of my mouth. How Vanessa and I had become friends, then more. How what I thought was love had grown between us. For years, I believed I'd found the woman I was meant to be with. After I met Cara and felt my fire burn for her so intensely, I realized how much of a blind fool I'd been back then. I let Vanessa get close to my family and me. Let her figure out our weaknesses and that my father had been ready to stand against Carridan and bring him down for using magic to manipulate the other princes.

"The day she turned on me," I said, my voice dropping to a whisper at this point in the story, "I thought I had to be dreaming. Or Carridan had her under a spell. And he did, just not a magical one. I let her get close, and my family paid the price for it."

"And? Calrod, she manipulated you. You're not the first male to be used by a woman like her."

"I shouldn't have let it happen."

Cara cupped my face, turning it so I had no choice, but to look at her. I expected to see anger or disappointment. Instead, the only emotion staring back at me from her gaze was the same overwhelming love I saw every morning when she woke up.

"You thought she loved you," she said. "She's the one who should carry the blame for what your family went through. Not you."

"If I hadn't gotten close, let her in..." I argued, tearing myself away from Cara and climbing to my feet. "I should've realized what she was planning, but I didn't. I failed my family. I'm the eldest son, and I destroyed my family's legacy."

"Is that really what you think?" She stood up, following me while I paced near the trees. "Arkon, Dagon, and you might've been chased out of the Underworld, but look what you found. All three of you found your mates. Arkon's having a baby with Jas. The three of you might not rule over some province in the Underworld anymore, but you've made Oak Hollow your home. And the people here, they've taken you in. All of you."

"They don't know us."

"They might not realize you're demons, but they know good people when they see them. And you, Calrod, are good. Just like your brothers." She slipped her arms around my sides and hugged me from behind. "You don't need to carry this shit around with you anymore. Vanessa's the traitor. She's the monster, not you. And I'll never let her hurt you again."

I spun around in her arms. "You are not to hunt her down, understand me?"

"Never said I would, but she's hurt you enough. You're my mate, Calrod. I'm going to make sure she can't touch you."

I believed her, too. That damn determination in her eyes set my blood on fire. I wasn't sure how she didn't hate me right now for putting her life in even more danger or how she wasn't as disappointed in me as I'd been with myself all these years.

"I don't deserve you," I whispered, running my thumb over her bottom lip.

"You do, and I'm not going anywhere. But you should tell your brothers the truth. It'll help ease the rest of that guilt you've been lugging around. And the sadness."

"What sadness?"

"I saw it in your eyes the first time we met. Made my own heart hurt."

"Great. Caused you pain the first day we met."

"I mean, to be fair, I sort of fell off of a ladder and landed on you, so I think we're even," she teased. She stood on her toes and kissed me, surrounding me with her love as Vanessa had never been able to do. "Tell them. They won't hate you for it."

I wasn't so sure, but I had to speak with them anyway. Vanessa's words and her being in town with an entourage of demons told me two things. The warding Cyrene had hoped would be enough clearly wasn't working against whatever magic Carridan and his minions wielded. And second, he wasn't simply after Arkon, Dagon, and me. He'd come to Oak Hollow searching for something more. Cyrene's odd behavior of late made me believe she had an idea of what that might be. Then again, maybe I did. Weston, the first demon to attack Cara, he'd called her a witch. Was it possible Carridan wasn't merely after her because she was with me? There were too many unanswered questions, each one leaving me more anxious than before.

Tonight, I'd warn my brothers that Vanessa was in town. Tomorrow, I'd call Cyrene and set up a family meeting. It was time the witch told us the truth, and far past time I let my brothers know how badly I'd screwed us all over.

THE STORM POUNDED the house with rain most of the night. Not that Cara and I slept much anyway. I'd barely get my rage under control, and it'd spike all over again. Too many horrible scenarios played out in my mind of how yesterday could've gone. Arkon and Dagon had been furious to hear Vanessa was here. Neither knew yet the situation was far worse than another of Carridan's loyal dogs showing up to set us on edge.

Why wasn't he simply attacking? Why threaten us or warn us? Nothing that bastard was doing right now made sense.

We were supposed to head to Cyrene's this evening, but the doorbell rang around seven in the morning. The storm had finally drifted to the east, and I went to see who was at the cottage. "Morgan? What are you doing here so early?"

She stepped inside, shaking out her jacket. "Sorry. Dagon said he needs you to check something out with him. He had a vision this morning, won't tell me what it was. I figured I'd stay with Cara while you go with him and check it out." She yawned, rubbing her eyes. "Got any coffee?"

"Just made a pot," Cara called from the kitchen. "Help yourself."

Morgan gave me a sleepy smile that did nothing to make me feel better and went to the kitchen, passing Cara on her way out.

"We'll be alright for a while," she assured me. "If Dagon needs you, you should go."

She was right. Dagon hadn't seen anything worthwhile in weeks. If he had a vision terrible enough he wasn't going to share it with Morgan, I had no doubt it had to do with Carridan. The idea of leaving left a pit in my stomach. Vanessa showing up yesterday had been a bad omen.

"I'll text you every ten minutes while you're gone," Cara said.

"Deal. I'll be back as quick as I can. Do not leave the house."

She kissed me, and I left, climbed into my truck, and sped through the wet streets across town to Dagon and Morgan's place. The second I parked my truck out front, fire pooled in my hands. The front door to their place had been broken open. Growling, I sprinted for the house, fire at the ready, but it appeared I was too late.

Dagon whirled around in a full rage, a bloody dagger gripped in his hand. "Calrod?"

Two dead demons lay on the floor of the destroyed living room. Blood spattered the walls and the ceiling. "The hell happened?"

"We were attacked, that's what happened," Morgan snapped.

I jerked around, shaking my head. "You! Why are you here?"

"I live here," Morgan replied. "You're afraid. What's wrong? Calrod?"

"You came to the house. You said Dagon needed me," I replied, my heart pounding. "Shit."

I grabbed my cell from my pocket, checking it for a text from Cara. There was one saying all was fine. I called her, waiting for her to answer. She had to get out of the house. When she didn't pick up, I cursed and bolted out the door. Dagon yelled after me, but there was no time to respond. I knew who was at the house with Cara.

Vanessa was going to die today. I was going to burn her alive and laugh at her rotting corpse for thinking she could come between my mate and me. I pushed my boot to the floorboard and floored it across town.

10

———

Cara

I set my phone down after texting Calrod. Morgan had a cup of coffee in hand and was walking around the living room. "You don't have any idea what Dagon saw?"

"No. He doesn't like to tell me everything."

I scoffed. "Sounds familiar."

She paused at the mantel, resting her fingers on the wood shelf beneath my newest sculpture. "This is fascinating. Where did you get this?"

I grinned, my cheeks burning. The piece she was looking at was the one Calrod's fire had managed to burn while we'd been wrapped in each other's arms. The twisted forms of the flames had taken on some interesting shapes, a strange combination of fire, and what I was starting to realize was the energy that passed between the two of us. It was like the fire and its ghost all in one.

"Uh, I made it the other morning," I explained. "I work with clay a lot."

"You truly are an intriguing woman," Morgan said, then laughed. "Pity."

The second that word left her lips, a chill shot down my spine. "What did you say?"

She grinned, but the wicked curl to her smile wasn't Morgan's. Her eyes flared with magic, and I staggered, fumbling to snag my cell phone off the couch. She screamed, beating me to it, and threw me into the far wall. I grunted from the impact. Something shimmery manifested beside the figure that was clearly not Morgan.

Beth. She was waving her arms and trying to give me a chance to recover. The last of the glamour fell away, and Vanessa let out a maniacal laugh, glaring at me.

"Pathetic. What does Calrod see in you?"

I flipped her off, waiting for Beth to gather enough energy to manifest into a more solid form. I inched across the wall, not sure where I planned on going.

"Enough," Vanessa snapped. Her hand shot to her right where Beth stood and closed around the spirit's neck as if she were a solid human being. She squeezed, and Beth's form thrashed, struggling to get free. Her body cracked and exploded in a shower of white mist, hovering in the air like fog. "Much better. Now, let's get on with how I'm going to torture you then kill you, shall we?"

Calrod was right. Vanessa was not someone to mess with. Too late now.

"Screw you, bitch."

She laughed, clapping her hands. "Such courage. It's going to be fun to tear you to pieces. Calrod will see then he was a fool to believe you were his mate. Sadly, I'm not allowed to kill you, but I'm quite practiced at ensuring my victims remain alive for all the excitement."

She leaped over the couch, and I met her with the standing lamp I snagged from the corner. I smashed her in the head with it. The pole bent, and she snarled, baring her fangs at me. She backhanded me, and I rolled from the living room into the kitchen. I tried to focus on the energy as Cyrene had taught me, but with Beth gone, it had been sucked right out of the house. Not that being transparent right now would do me any good. Vanessa had grabbed Beth and destroyed her with one touch.

I scrambled through the kitchen, debating on grabbing a knife. I doubted that'd help either. My cell started ringing in the other room. Calrod. He'd be here soon, I knew he would. All I had to do was stay alive until then. That wasn't so hard, right?

I was at the garage door, ready to try and barricade myself out there, but an invisible rope snagged me around my middle and dragged me back.

"We haven't had any fun yet," Vanessa purred. "I want to hear all about your time with Calrod. Tell me, is he still a fantastic lover?"

Trying not to freak out, I smirked and forced a laugh. "Better with me than he was with you."

Her lip twitched, and her eyes narrowed. "I doubt that."

"Really? He burns for me, Vanessa. Did he ever do that for you? Did his fire ever wrap around you and make you forget the rest of the world was even there? It does that for me. He's mine. He's always been mine. You were just an unfortunate steppingstone."

The rope around me tightened, and I gasped, fighting not falling over or passing out.

"You don't deserve him," I rasped, noticing her

hands starting to shake. "You never did, and you're going to die for hurting him."

"And who's going to hurt me? You?"

"I'm not just going to hurt you," I warned. "I'm going to kill you. I promised I would, remember?"

"You are nothing," she snapped. "How about I prove it?"

I wasn't even sure what drove me to do it, but I sensed new energy in the house. Vanessa's. Using her own magic against her, I snatched the ghost of her power hovering in the air and directed it right back at her.

A bright burst of white light flooded the kitchen. She screamed, stumbling, and I took my chance, sprinting out of the house and into the yard. White splotches in my eyes left me half-blind. I shook my head, then rubbed my eyes, willing my vision to clear. I considered taking off into the woods, but the notion of running from this demon who caused Calrod so much turmoil had my bare feet digging into the muddied ground.

A light misty rain was still falling, leftover from the storm that had rolled over the town this morning. The air was charged. The remnants of the thunder and lightning made the hairs on my arm stand up.

I shut my eyes, tapping into that steady flow of energy ready and waiting to be used. Cyrene had said most natural events left behind residual energy. She hadn't told me how alive it would feel or formidable. I held my hands out to my sides, palms open and ready to receive the energy.

"You should've run," Vanessa snarled, crashing through the back door.

I didn't bother looking, too busy focusing on the ghost of the storm pulsing through the open air. It called to me silently, just as the spirits did.

"Did you hear me? You're going to regret everything."

A crackling sound met my ears, but I still didn't look. The raindrops that had been lightly brushing across my face grew, their cold touch coming faster and faster. More rain pattered the ground around me, and the wind kicked up.

"What are you doing?" Vanessa demanded. "Your magic won't work against me."

I finally opened my eyes, doing my best to hide my shock at the sight that awaited me. Rain swirled around me like a cocoon. The clouds over-head had darkened, and the wind gusted through the trees, battering my cottage. They were strong enough to push Vanessa. Thunder rumbled, but it sounded far off, as if I was hearing it through a wall.

"You won't win this fight," Vanessa shouted to be heard over the howling wind. She clutched at the pendant hanging from the silver chain around her neck. Briefly, I wondered if that was why Calrod's fire hadn't been able to touch her.

No matter. This wasn't simple magic coming for her. This was a storm, and I was at the heart of it. Not just the heart of it. No, I was the storm, just as Calrod always said. A bolt of lightning flashed across my vision and struck Vanessa.

A shimmering shield blocked it from hitting her, but I wasn't even close to giving up. She yelled, but a second strike and a third drove her to her knees, her magic protecting her trembling from the impacts. The lightning crackled through the air while thunder shattered the air. I moved forward, driving the storm into Vanessa.

She screamed, straining to push me back, but even her magic couldn't withstand the force of mother nature.

Not even its ghost.

The wind's fury drowned out her shouts. I raised my right hand over my head, the storm's energy coursing through my veins. Lightning crackled at my fingertips, and I directed the power right at Vanessa. The magical shield exploded outward, and the bolt struck home. Her arms flew to her sides and her back arched while she was forced to remain on her knees. Her body was scorched, but she wasn't dead, not yet. I'd promised her that much. I wasn't about to go back on my word.

The lightning built in ferocity. I unleashed it all at Vanessa. She screamed while the electricity shot through her body. Unable to contain the burst of energy, jolts jumped from her, striking the ground and the house behind her. When the lightning stopped, her body was charred, scorched to cinder. There were no eyes in the sockets anymore. She toppled to the side, bits of her burnt flesh sloughing off. The storm's energy left me, and I sagged forward, falling to all fours in the mud.

"Cara?"

Through my blurry vision, I thought I spotted Calrod. His fire surrounded me.

"Told you," I whispered. "I'll always protect you, too." I fell into his waiting arms and passed out.

"THEY'RE WATCHING the farmhouse and the shop, too," Arkon said, the amber aura around him as bright as his eyes. "We can't go back to Oak Hollow."

I wasn't surprised to hear that news. I shifted on the couch, and Calrod adjusted the pillows behind my back without me asking. He tugged the fleece blanket up higher, too, then pressed his palm to my forehead, his lips thinning.

"Fever's gone," he murmured.

"Good," I said through a yawn. "See? Nothing to worry about."

He tucked the blanket in around me more, then lightly ran his fingers through my hair. I'd been laying on this couch for the last few hours, longer, I guessed, since this was where I came to. After Calrod had returned to the house, he, Morgan, and Dagon had brought me to Cyrene's place. We'd been hanging out in the library that looked more like a comfortable sitting room now. My legs were draped over his lap, and according to the others, he hadn't moved until I'd opened my eyes. So many questions swirled in those dark blue depths, and I hadn't had answers for any of them. I remembered what occurred at the cottage, what I'd done to kill Vanessa. The use of so much magic so fast was what left me exhausted and with a slight fever. Cyrene had assured us it was normal. Calrod's grunt of annoyance had been enough for me to know he wasn't happy to find me in that state.

He'd been furious with himself for letting Vanessa trick him so easily. But hey, she'd tricked me, too, the bitch. Not that it mattered now. She was dead.

But the story of what she did to Calrod had needed to be told. He'd confessed everything to Dagon and Arkon. The silence that followed was heavy. He'd said he'd accept whatever they thought or did to him. His brothers had walked over and smacked him upside the head for being an idiot and thinking they'd disown him.

All these years, he'd carried around unnecessary guilt, believing his brothers would turn on him for being manipulated. Vanessa had tricked them all. None had known her loyalties had been with Carridan. I'd given Calrod a brief, "I told you so" look that he'd quickly kissed off my face. The guilt and sorrow that had been in his eyes since the first time I met him were finally slipping away and replaced with the love growing like a fire between us.

I turned my head toward Calrod's hand, and his fingers brushed my cheek. I smiled softly, letting my eyes close, too tired still to keep them open. But I wasn't too tired to listen.

While Vanessa had come after me, three more demons had tried to kill Dagon and Morgan at their place. They'd finished them off by the time Calrod arrived and realized what was happening. It'd been safe to assume more would've tried to hurt Jasmine and Arkon. The second we'd all shown up, Arkon and Dagon had taken off with Rik to check out the antique store and the farmhouse. From the way Arkon couldn't stop twitching and pacing around, they'd done more than simply show up to watch. Morgan cringed every few seconds, clearly picking up on his emotions.

Jasmine whispered his name, but he only stilled after she got up out of her chair and caught his hand. "Whatever they did to the house, to the shop, it doesn't matter," she told him sternly.

He hung his head, sighing. "You're right. I'm sorry, I just, I wanted you to be safe. Both of you and now, I have no idea what's going to happen."

She cupped his face, forcing him to look at her. "We are safe because we have you."

"The baby has both of us," he reminded her, and she scoffed.

"Yeah, because I'm oh so powerful right now. Not

like I can use people's energies against them or turn into a damn storm," she said, turning to look at Morgan and me. "I wish I could've seen it."

Calrod's quiet growl vibrated through the couch. "I'm not even sure how to describe any of it."

"It was fun," I said, and his brow arched while he scowled. "What? It was. I was a storm for those few moments, and damn, just feeling that energy still makes me jittery." I sat up more, some of the exhaustion fading. "And you are not powerless," I added to Jasmine.

"She's right," Cyrene said, poking her head back into the room, with Rik right behind her. She had several large books in her hands and set them down with a loud thud on the black wood-carved coffee table in the center of the room. "I don't know why you keep doubting me."

Jasmine crossed her arms atop her pregnant belly. "I haven't done anything magical. At all."

Cyrene laughed. "And what do you call creating a child with Arkon, hmm? That is magic, Jasmine. I don't think you understand how hard it is for a demon to have a child with someone who isn't a demon."

"So what, I'm just a baby maker?"

Cyrene sighed and went to her. "You are far more

than that. I was trying not to add to your stress level, at the request of Arkon, but I can see now I should've simply told you this months ago."

"Told me what?" Jasmine asked while the rest of us perked up, too.

"You have always had magic in your veins, just as Morgan and Cara have, but after your first encounter with our world, it tucked itself away," Cyrene explained. "Magic isn't merely energy that we can manipulate. It feels and thinks as much as we do. It saw what you were going through, and it went into a hibernation of sorts until you were ready."

Jasmine glanced to Arkon, but he shrugged. "But why haven't I seen it yet? With everything that's going on, it should've woken up by now, right?"

"It might have if you hadn't become pregnant. Right now, your magic is busy helping you create a very unique life." Cyrene waited for Jasmine's nod, then rested her hand on her stomach. "Your baby will be strong because of the magic in both of you. Once your child comes into the world, your magic will return to you, of that I'm certain."

"Don't know why you're in such a hurry to have your magic back anyway," Arkon muttered.

"Why do you think? I protected you before I was pregnant, remember?"

"Oh, I do, vividly," he growled in reply. "I'm not keen on seeing that again."

Jasmine patted his cheek and grinned. "I'd say I'm sorry, but I'm not. We're in this shit together, remember? It's what I do. What we all do," she said, nodding toward Morgan and me.

Arkon said something in reply, but it was too quiet for me to hear. Cyrene returned to the books on the table and flipped through the top one. "Was this the amulet you saw the demon wearing during the first attack?" she asked Calrod.

He leaned forward to study the sketch of the red stone amulet. "Yeah, that'd be it."

Cyrene's face darkened while she pulled out a second book and turned to another page. "And you said Vanessa was wearing something around her neck, too. Was it this?" she asked me.

I tilted my head, straining to recall the details of the necklace I'd barely glimpsed. "I think so."

"What's wrong?" Morgan asked, studying Cyrene with a frown. "You're afraid."

Cyrene shut her eyes, visibly gathering herself. "Prince Carridan isn't simply coming after you all with his minions. He's giving them powerful arti-facts, some that have been lost for centuries. From the sound of it, you two destroyed these," she said to

Calrod and me. "But I doubt they're the only ones his soldiers will be using to bring you down."

"That's bad, right?" I asked. "Calrod wasn't able to use his fire against Vanessa or that other demon. What could the others do?"

"Terrible things," Cyrene whispered, and a cold breeze blew through the room. The candle flames flickered, and the fire that had been burning happily away in the hearth sputtered, threatening to go out. "Carridan shouldn't have been able to get his hands on these without the rest of the magical world hearing about it." She paced across the room, the wind kicking up with each step she took. "I don't think those demons tracking you the same time Soul Piercer showed up were a coincidence," she whispered, whipping around and nailing Arkon with a fierce look.

"You think he's planning something else," Calrod said, sitting forward. "What? A takeover of the Underworld? Why waste time coming after us?"

"Everything about this feels odd," Arkon added. "Has from the beginning. If he wanted us dead, why not simply charge into Oak Hollow and wipe us all out? He's got the manpower to do it."

"He's after something," Dagon chimed in. "That has to be it."

"But there aren't any other artifacts in town. You would've sensed them by now," Arkon said to Cyrene. "You checked after we found Soul Piercer."

"If I had more answers, I'd give them to you," Cyrene said, but Morgan's eyes narrowed.

Cyrene wasn't telling us everything. She appeared almost nervous and wouldn't meet any of our gazes. Whatever else was going on, she had to sense it or had seen it somehow. Her violet eyes flicked to me then away, but that second was all I needed to know I was right.

"Doesn't really matter, does it?" Dagon said. "If he's after something or not. We know he's here for us, and that's what we need to focus on. Keeping our asses alive and stopping him."

"He's right," Jasmine said. "We can't stay with Cyrene forever."

"So you what, want to make a plan to go after him?" Arkon asked hotly.

"I want us to get back to our lives," she argued. "I don't think that's too much to ask."

"We don't even know if he's surfaced yet," Calrod told her. "And there's no way to know how many demons or witches or whatever else is working for him are in Oak Hollow. If we make a move, the wrong move, he won't hesitate to attack the town. He'll slaughter innocents without blinking an eye."

"Then we lure him away from town," I said, shrugging. "Have him come after us somewhere else. A place we pick. Ambush him or something."

"Ambush him or something?" Calrod repeated. "And who said anything about a 'we'?"

"I just used a storm to kill Vanessa. I can do it again."

Calrod rolled his eyes toward the ceiling. "You haven't even recovered yet, and you're already talking about going after a demon prince of the Underworld."

"I don't see the problem."

"Of course you don't," he uttered. "We're not talking about this, not while you can't even stand up on your own yet."

Tossing the blanket aside, I pushed myself upright the rest of the way, scooted to the edge of the cushion, and stood up. I gave him a triumphant smile until my knees wobbled, and I crashed right back down, a wave of dizziness making me grab my head.

"You were saying?" Calrod asked.

"Bite me," I replied and scrunched my eyes shut, waiting for the spinning to stop.

"It's been a long couple of days, and the ones to follow will be the same," Cyrene said. "I suggest you get some rest while you can. We can work out a plan of action tomorrow."

I wanted to argue, but Calrod had already scooped me into his arms and exited the library. I was going to tell him I could walk, but he was too warm. I sighed, relaxing into him and enjoying being this close while I could.

We reached what was our room now on the second floor, and he pushed open the door. The room was decked out in shades of violet and green. Vines covered the walls, dotted with white and iridescent flowers. They curled up the ceiling, too, and hung over the black four-poster bed. There was a stone fireplace to the right and a small sitting area with violet overstuffed chairs in front of it.

"Cyrene's Bed & Breakfast," I said with a grin.

Calrod didn't smile when set me on the edge of the bed. "You should get some sleep."

"And where are you going? Off to secretly plan behind my back with your brothers?"

He stilled halfway to the door. "No."

"Yeah, you are." I sighed, fiddling with the black bedspread. "I'm sorry I scared you today."

He whirled around. "You think you scared me?"

"I mean with the whole Vanessa attacking and my turning into a storm. Yeah, pretty sure it terrified you."

"Why are you apologizing? You didn't ask her to come after you," he ranted.

"No, that's true."

He came to me, kneeling on the floor, and caught my hands. "The notion that I could've lost you today does terrify me, but I'm in awe of you, Cara. What you can do? What I witnessed at the cottage? You are far more formidable than I gave you credit for."

"Which is why I can help you fight Carridan."

"No," he snapped.

"Yes," I argued just as fiercely. "You heard Cyrene. Carridan's probably got more of these artifacts and whatnot. I was able to get around the amulet Vanessa wore."

"And what if it hadn't stormed this morning? What energy would you have used then?"

"Whatever I have to." I squeezed his hands, not letting him pull away, though he tried. "I can practice with your fire more. If you're using it during the fight, I can tap into that."

His thumb immediately brushed over the place where I'd burned my hand. Worry swirled in his eyes, and he hesitated. Our time together had been punctuated by one terrifying moment after the next. And now we were sitting here talking about essentially going to war with a demon prince from the Underworld. The weight of what I was asking him to let me do shone in his shimmering eyes, and I mentally kicked myself. We had no idea when the next attack would come or how much time we had before Carridan forced our hand.

I was going to spend every second of those hours reminding Calrod of what we had together and that he wasn't alone.

I pulled him to me, kissing him. I tugged his shirt over his head, then planted my hands on his chest. Fire immediately surrounded us, and he lifted me into his arms, climbing onto the bed with me. Our touches were languid while we shed the rest of our clothes. I pressed my naked body to him, taking his heat and relishing in the flames that flowed over my skin. I gripped his hardened shaft in my palms, loving how it pulsed and swelled even more. I rolled Calrod to his back and straddled him. I eased myself onto his cock while we trembled from the connection. He massaged my ass, moving his hips in time with mine while I rode him, slow and steady.

The words I wanted to say to him were right on my lips, but I couldn't give them sound. Calrod sat up, gently maneuvering my legs, so they stretched out behind him. Not once did our bodies part.

"I know, love," he whispered against my lips. "I know."

We moved as one person, kissing and touching while we rocked together, finding that perfect moment of bliss. He buried his face in my neck, groaning with his release. His hips bucked one final time, and I squeezed him tightly within my sheath. This was more than love, what we had between us. This was destiny, fate, some cosmic alignment, whatever. This was where I was meant to be and who I was meant to be with.

No demon prince was going to change that.

11

———

Calrod

Back in the library at Cyrene's house, the quiet of the early morning hours hung heavy in the air. Arkon, Dagon, and I had managed to sneak out of our rooms and meet down here, hoping to come up with some semblance of a plan for our next move. Unfortunately, after several hours of talking, arguing, and talking some more, we realized Cara's idea about setting an ambush was our best and only option at this point.

We'd come up with the best way to draw Carridan out of Oak Hollow, but not tonight. Or, well, this morning. I had my hands on the wooden mantel, leaning over while I stared into the remaining embers of the dying fire. I still had too many questions, but all I wanted right then was to get back upstairs to Cara.

"I'm getting some sleep," Dagon murmured, patting me on the shoulder, then Arkon on his back on his way out the door. "Night."

Arkon joined me at the fireplace, his brow crinkled and his eyes shimmering in the dimness of the library. "You think we can pull off a plan like this and live?"

"What choice do we have?"

"No good ones, not anymore." He grunted, and I straightened, eyeing my brother. "Cyrene returned Soul Piercer to me."

"Guess she believes you need it."

"She's not telling us everything. You saw her face while we spoke earlier. Do you think Carridan's after her, too?"

"She wouldn't be the first powerful witch he went after or added to his collection." I dug my claws into the mantel, and the embers in the hearth crackled, bursting with new life in the face of my growing ire.

I'd heard the stories about Carridan's dungeons, as had my brothers and so many others. Dungeons filled with supernatural beings he'd collected over the years. He'd use them for their power, then toss them aside, selling them on the black market or killing them. He would've kept my brothers and me in those same dungeons if we hadn't escaped when we did. The more my thoughts drifted to those dark days, the more I tried to understand how he'd been able to trick the princes into believing our father had been the villain. What could he possibly have in his possession that was strong enough to hold sway over so many princes for this long?

"Sorry," Arkon said, shaking me from the rabbit hole my mind had fallen into. "You should get some rest, too."

I wasn't sure that was possible. I waited for him to leave, then took one last look at the fire. If only I'd waited to find Cara until after Carridan was destroyed. Fear of losing her wouldn't be so prevalent then. The fire that burned so hot inside me grew cold, imagining the coming days without her in them.

Seeing her become the literal embodiment of a storm had been awe-inspiring and terrifying at the same time. Lightning had flashed in her eyes. It had listened to her commands. The image of her wrapped in the howling winds and rain was one I'd never forget. She could be extremely fearsome if given time and a chance to hone her abilities, but it was too soon to think she'd stand against Carridan and win. Too damn soon.

With a growl, I pushed off the mantel, intending to go upstairs, but Cyrene's raised voice caught my ear. She was in the saloon, and I headed that way, keeping my steps quiet.

"—need to listen to me," Cyrene said, her voice shaking with desperation. "I can't stop what's going to happen, and you can't be here. Not anymore. We've stayed together far longer than we should've, and you know that as much as I do."

"Do I look like I give a damn?" a deep voice asked.

Rik? I'd never heard the fae speak until now. Whereas Cyrene's voice was filled with frantic energy, his was fury.

He continued, "You can't ask this of me. I won't do it, and you should know that by now."

"I don't want this for you," Cyrene argued.

"That's not your choice to make. It never was."

"Triksar—"

"No," Rik snapped. "I'm not having this conversation with you again. This is my destiny, as yours is to ensure magic doesn't die. To guarantee the darkness you've sensed for centuries will be stopped."

His words rooted me to the floor. What darkness? Magic was dying? What was he talking about?

There was a shuffling of steps, what I thought was Cyrene still quietly pleading with Rik, then the fae came storming out of the saloon. He acted as if he didn't even see me and walked on by. A door slammed down the hall somewhere behind me. I hesitated, wondering if I should turn around or stay. A crash came from the saloon, and I hurried through the slated, swinging doors. Cyrene stood in the center of the space, one of the tables on its side before her. She had her back to me, her shoulders rapidly rising and falling. Violet lights gleamed at her fingertips.

"You alright?" I asked, and she flinched.

"Calrod, I didn't hear you come in." She cleared her throat and flipped her long locks over her shoulder. "And yes, I'm fine. Perfectly fine."

"The argument you just had with Rik would say otherwise."

She glared over her shoulder at me, then sighed, her face crumbling. "Demons aren't the only ones who can be ungodly stubborn and overprotective."

"You want to talk about it?"

"I appreciate the gesture, but from that look in your eyes, you have enough on your mind as it is."

She looked to the table, shaking her head. She was muttering under her breath in a language I didn't understand but let it go.

I went to the table and righted it, picking up the chairs she'd knocked over with it.

"Thank you, Calrod," she murmured. "And for what it's worth, I'm sorry."

I stilled, my hackles rising, wondering if she was going to finally admit she'd been hiding shit from us. "About what?"

"So many things," she whispered.

"What's going on, really?" I pushed. "What haven't you told us? Why did Rik say magic was dying? Cyrene, what have you seen? Just tell us."

"That, I'm afraid, is a conversation for another day," she replied, then rushed to me, squeezing my arm in a steely grip. "No matter what happens, swear to me you will keep living. Not surviving, Calrod, but living, for yourself, for Cara. For all of you. No more hiding behind a wall of sorrow and guilt. There's no more room for those emotions, understand me?"

I wanted to argue until she told me the damn truth, but the glint in her eyes had me biting back my frustration. I covered her hand with mine, nodding. "I swear it. Cyrene," I started, but she backed away, moving toward the door. "I'm sorry we're bringing this mess to your door," I said anyway while she stood on the threshold, the swinging door partly open.

"You're not. Carridan would've come for me eventually."

"Why? Just to add you to his collection?"

She tilted her head, the violet in her eyes glowing for the briefest second. "Something like that. Rest while you can, Calrod. I'll see you in the morning."

The doors swung shut behind her for a few seconds, then finally came to a muffled stop. The lingering anguish from Cyrene's argument with Rik permeated the air. It seeped into my skin, right down to my very bones. I stopped wondering about what other secrets had yet to be revealed, turned around, and rushed out of the saloon. I was outside the door to Cara's and my room a few seconds later. Quietly, I opened the door, shutting it softly behind me. Cara was in bed, the blankets pooled around her waist. She'd fallen asleep naked, and I was graced with her beauty once again. She lay on her stomach, hugging a pillow. Her hair was wild around her head. She had a sleepy smile on her face, and my heart stuttered.

I slipped out of my clothes, peeled back the

covers, and slid in beside her. She mumbled, her legs shifting. She rolled to her side, resting her back to my chest while she slept on. I moved her hair back and kissed her temple. My hand wandered down her side, lightly squeezing her hip before shifting to her thigh. I closed my eyes, content to simply fall asleep with her safe in my arms.

When her hand closed around my shaft, my eyes opened wide. I glanced down to see her grinning, the wrinkles at her eyes telling me she wasn't asleep like I thought. Lazily, her hand pumped down my length, and I kissed her shoulder, then her neck. I was going to tell her she should just go back to sleep, but she rolled over and pinned me to the bed, a mischievous gleam in her eyes. While she lay atop me, I cupped her face, brushing my thighs over her cheeks. Fire seeped from my palms. Ribbons of flames soon covered her, and she leaned down, pressing her lips to mine for a kiss that ignited the wild passion I had for her and always would.

Our tongues danced, and the fire glowed brighter, blue and white flames lighting up the bedroom. She slipped her way down my body, leaving a trail of kisses along my sternum, then lower. She nibbled my hip, raking her nails down my thighs. She licked up my shaft, and I growled. She winked, then closed her mouth around my cock, just the tip, and sucked hard and fast. My growl turned into a groan, and the flames immediately condensed lower on her body. They shifted between her thighs, and she moaned around my shaft. Her eyes became hooded with unquenched desire. I chuckled until she had me back in her mouth and me nearly begging for mercy. Watching her suck me off had me sitting up long enough to maneuver her around so I could ravish her sex with my mouth and fire.

The flames condensed then penetrated her sheath, filling her while I massaged her clit, then lavished her sex with my tongue. Her nails dug into my thigh, and she took even more of me in. I couldn't get enough of her after that. I sensed my release creeping toward that moment of no return. I moved my hips to the side, and she lost her hold on me. She protested, but the words cut off. I filled her with my fingers, pumping them in hard and fast while she cursed, and her body trembled.

Her pleasure spilled over my fingers and her inner muscles throbbed, frantic to keep me inside her. I rolled her to her back and covered her with my body. She was panting, and I kissed her, loving how her legs instantly wrapped around my waist. She grabbed my horns while I massaged my way down her thighs to her ass then back again. We rolled in the bed again, tangling the blankets until I shoved them away with an annoyed grunt that had her laughing. All the while, the blue and white flames shifted from her body to mine and back again, never faltering.

At some point, I caught her hands and held them over her head while the fire slipped to her sheath once more. She bit her lip, and the second the flames filled her, she cried out, her back arching off the bed. I captured her nipple in my mouth, suckling that tender nub of flesh while she writhed beneath me. I shifted her to her stomach, kissing her spine and not letting the fire stop. She fisted her hands in the sheets, shoving her ass into the cradle of my body. I knew what she wanted, but this was too enjoyable to watch to stop now.

I found that tender bead and massaged it. She pushed her ass against my cock, rubbing against it. She glanced over her shoulder the second she came apart again. For that moment, all I saw in her eyes was the ghost of the storm she'd become.

The air in the room grew heavy with the impending conflict and what we might lose. What she might have to become for us to survive. She spun around the same time I went to hug her close, and we ended up on the bed, unable to touch each other enough. She straddled me once more, and then she had me buried in her sheath. We sighed at the connection that shot through our bodies. My fire met the lightning I was sure had become a permanent part of her.

All I wanted for the rest of my days was Cara like this. With me, safe and alive, her heart pounding and her eyes alight with life and love. The fire pulsed larger, cocooning us in the blaze that was everything I felt for Cara and more. She'd proved who she was, that she'd kill to protect me.

That she'd fight by my side no matter the risk or the cost to herself. Cyrene made me swear to keep living. The only way to do that was to kill Carridan. If Cara's magic helped me reach that end, I had to accept going into that battle with her.

Her head fell back with a cry that shattered the fear threatening to wind its way through my very soul. My groan joined hers, and I held myself inside her, willing her to see the same future I saw for us. She collapsed atop me, both of us breathing harshly. The fires flickered and went out, and I rolled us over, keeping her beneath me.

"I'd ask what's on your mind, but I think I know."

She mussed the hair around my horns. "We're going to make it. You'll see."

"I know we will. I have you beside me. As much as I don't want you to fight, I need you."

Her brow arched. "Well, where did this optimism come from?"

"Where do you think?" I nuzzled her neck, and she laughed, squirming. Staying in bed all morning sounded great to me. It'd be a while until the others got up anyway. I doubted either of my brothers had fallen asleep so quickly.

I was just about to slowly fill Cara again—

A harsh scream cut through the house.

We looked to the door then were rushing to get up and grab clothes.

A second scream was followed by a door slamming open and Arkon's yell for Cyrene. I followed Cara out the door. Dagon and Morgan exited their room, too, and we hurried to the guest room at the end of the hall. T

he door was open, and Arkon stood beside the bed, clutching Jasmine's hand.

"Early," Jasmine was repeating. "It's too early. Something's wrong."

"It's going to be alright," Arkon whispered,

smoothing her hair from her face and clutching her hand.

Cyrene rushed into the room, her blank face doing nothing to ease the tension emanating from Arkon and Jasmine. She started to speak but clutched at her stomach. She wasn't the only one. Morgan and Cara mirrored her, the three of them doubling over as if in too much pain to stand upright.

Cyrene cursed, staggering toward the windows just as Rik ran in to join us. Whatever she'd been about to say cut off in a gasp. She toppled forward, with Rik barely catching her in time. Cara collapsed next, falling to her knees, taking me with her. Morgan was cursing, her hand fisted in Dagon's shirt. What the hell was happening? I was about to yell my question, but a thunderous boom shook the house. A second one came with an ear-splitting crack that sent a sharp jolt of energy rippling painfully down my spine.

Cara's gasp of pain told me she'd felt it, too.

"No," Arkon whispered, then snarled, glaring toward the windows. "The warding."

My heart plummeted. Carridan was here. Cara's grip on my hand tightened, and we looked to Jasmine and Arkon. Her hands closed protectively over her stomach, her eyes wide in panic. Arkon's muscles bulged, and his face shifted with the rage exploding out of him.

"Calrod," Cara rasped. "This feels wrong."

She was clutching at her stomach, her face twisted in confusion. A glowing circle appeared on the floor around her, the edges etched in symbols I didn't recognize. I hauled her into my arms. A bright flash of gold light blinded me, and I was clinging to nothing but air.

She was gone.

"Cara," I whispered, then shouted for her. There was no answer.

The same circle appeared beneath Morgan, and she was the next to disappear. Dagon bellowed, madly spinning around, searching for her. I caught Cyrene's gaze a moment before she was stolen from Rik, too.

"Arkon." Jasmine wrapped her arms tighter around her pregnant belly, a golden glow emanating from beneath the bed. She shouted for him. He fell forward onto the bed—

Jasmine vanishing right out from under him.

He snarled, tearing his claws through the bedding as if somehow, Jasmine would be there. He threw the bed clear across the room, his chest heaving while his nostrils flared.

"Why don't you come out and join us," a voice called from outside. "We have so much to talk about, don't you think?"

"Carridan," Arkon spat. "He has Jas and our baby, Calrod."

I grabbed my brother by the shoulders. "He won't get his hands on your child. We got out there, and we finish this. He'll not take anyone else from us."

"You're right," Arkon replied in a growl. "I'm going to rip his head off first."

12

Cara

My stomach rebelled, and I heaved. Nothing but bile came up, and I wasn't the only one. To my right, I heard Morgan's curse, and to my left came Cyrene's furious shout. I prayed I was wrong when I saw another flash of blinding gold light. A quick glance upward, and my gut twisted into even worse knots. Jasmine was lying on her side, her face etched in pain.

I shook my head, working to clear away the fuzziness left behind from whatever just happened to us. The same circle that had appeared around me inside burned into the ground now. I scrambled to get away from the symbols. My shoulders struck something solid, though there was nothing behind me except air. I shot my hand to the side, but it too hit an invisible barrier trapping me in the circle.

Jasmine groaned, and I turned, fear strangling me.

"Jas," I whispered, wishing I could reach her.

She was on all fours, digging her fingers into the mud. "The baby," she gasped, "she's coming."

We had to get out of here. We had to get her inside.

"Well, now, isn't this a marvelous morning. Here I thought I was merely tracking down three bastards needing execution, but what do I find instead? A house full of witches."

Slowly, I shifted my gaze and tensed. The demon who'd spoken wasn't alone, oh no, not even close. The gravel drive and grassy field outside Cyrene's house were lined with demons. Twenty, if not more. The one in front had spoken, and I turned my full attention to him.

He had glistening gold and copper horns that shone in the sunlight, barely peeking over the horizon. The smile that stretched his mouth sent a rush of ice shooting down my spine. He was lean at the waist, but his open button-down linen shirt was tight over his shoulders and biceps. The ivory shirt beneath completed his ensemble. He looked like he was headed to the yacht instead of resembling a prince here to kill us. He was even barefoot. His eyes shimmered gold, matching the aura around his body.

Carridan, this had to be him. He glanced at each of us in turn, then walked to Cyrene, trapped in a circle just like the rest of us. "My, you have only grown more beautiful over the decades." His voice was like paper rustling together, and it made my skin crawl.

Cyrene remained silent, her face expressionless. The tense silence was shattered by Jasmine's shout of pain.

Carridan drifted to her, crouching in front of her.

"My dear, it appears you're in labor. I do have perfect timing."

"Fuck you," Jasmine shouted, then screamed again, wrapping her arm tightly around her middle.

Carridan's greedy grin had me pushing against the barrier, wanting to get free. He chuckled, moved around us, and looked to the house. "Why don't you come out and join us? We have so much to talk about, don't you think?"

No, this wasn't how the fight was meant to go. We

were supposed to have a plan, and Jasmine wasn't supposed to be here. I pushed against the barrier, focusing on finding a way through it. It was magic. Energy. Maybe Morgan could destroy it somehow. She shouted curses, smashing her fist against it, but whatever had been used to create these walls held. Not even Cyrene was able to get through. She smashed her palms to the magical barrier. It shimmered but didn't fall.

Carridan continued to laugh as if he were having the best time ever right now. He probably was. Sick bastard. What was he going to do with us after he killed the brothers? Fear threatened to cloud my mind, but I wouldn't let it, not now. I'd told Calrod I was ready to fight, and I was. I had to be. We were getting out of this fight alive.

The front door to the house was no longer hidden behind Cyrene's glamour. The entire two stories were visible now, as was the fact that the house was clearly not a shack. Calrod led the way outside, fire swirling around his hands. Arkon and Dagon flanked him, followed by Rik.

The fae had changed in appearance as much as Calrod and his brothers had. I'd never thought he could look terrifying, but that's what he was at that moment. The tattoos on his body moved with a life of their own. His glowing eyes were filled with the intent to kill, and the double set of fangs in his mouth sent a shiver down my spine.

"Isn't this better, all of us being together?" Carridan said, spreading his arms.

Calrod's eyes flicked to me, and his growl reverberated off the trees. Four of them against Carridan and his demons. I didn't like those odds, not if we were trapped inside these damn circles. Carridan took a step closer, tilting his head.

"Well, now, I thought that was you." Carridan raised his right hand, and the sunlight glinted off a golden armband encrusted with rubies at his forearm. He snapped his fingers, and Rik's arms were forced to his sides. Dagon held onto him, but the pull of Carridan's magic was too strong. Rik was torn away from the house and landed right in front of the demon prince. "Still with the witch after all this time."

"Don't you touch him," Cyrene snapped.

Carridan winked at her, then lashed out, his hand wrapping around Rik's throat. "I warned him, the next time I saw him, it'd be his last on this earth for keeping you from me." His grip tightened.

Rik's eyes bulged. Cyrene was shouting, and Carridan released Rik, letting him fall to the ground.

"But you're right. Perhaps his death can wait a few minutes longer. I do have other business to tend to." Carridan whirled around and reached for Cyrene's arm.

She tried to yank it back, but he was too strong. He curled his right hand around her arm. Smoke emanated from it, and Cyrene gasped. Rik hissed from where he'd collapsed to the ground, but he was trapped, just like the rest of us. Calrod took a step forward, but Carridan's demons closed in, holding him back at sword point.

"It's all coming together," Carridan mused, releasing Cyrene.

Burned into her skin was a symbol. It looked like a twisted U with several smaller symbols jutting out around it and with what looked like roots coming out the bottom. Was it supposed to be a tree? I didn't recognize it.

Cyrene, however, looked panicked. Carridan happily danced his way from Cyrene to Morgan and did the same to her. Dagon bellowed in demonic, pushing forward as far as he could. Morgan shouted at him to stay back, her words cut off on a sharp cry, then Carridan released her, too. He went to Jasmine next, crouching to be at her level. She had broken out in a sweat and was groaning and cursing. He reached inside, and she raked her nails down his arm. He shoved her to her side. Arkon threw himself into the demons. Two of them snagged his arms and forced him to his knees. A sword appeared at his throat.

"Such a pleasant surprise to see you with child," Carridan said and snagged Jasmine's arm. "Don't worry, she'll be well looked after."

Jasmine's words disappeared beneath a scream. From the burn or the labor pains, I couldn't tell. I hit the ground, digging at the symbols in the dirt, praying they'd break somehow. Nothing I did worked, and I cursed Carridan for the evil asshole he was.

A set of bare feet appeared in front of me. "Your turn."

I glared up at the demon, refusing to get off my knees. I flipped him off, and he barked a laugh.

"Ah, I see it now. You must be the one who killed my sweet Vanessa."

"Yeah, I am. You want to die the same way?"

"Such fight in you. I can see why Calrod was drawn to you. You'll have a chance to show me what resides inside you, my dear Cara. We'll have all the time in the world once you're mine."

"I'll never be yours, dickhead."

His hand grabbed me by the throat and yanked me closer until our faces were inches away. "You will be mine. All of you. How you choose to be mine is your option. I suggest you give in." His right hand closed around my left arm. My skin burned, but I refused to let him know I was in pain. I bit my cheek, swallowing back the cry that wanted to break free of my mouth.

I had to do something. There had to be a way to get out of this mess. Energy. Tap into the energy. I focused on what was around me as Cyrene had been teaching me and stilled. I knew that cold sensation, though I'd told myself I'd never use it again. Dying might be the only way to throw Carridan off and give us a chance at living. I shut my eyes, praying Calrod would figure out what I was doing. My body grew cold, and I slumped forward.

"The pain's not that terrible," Carridan said, giving me a little shake.

I hardly felt it and my body went limp. The same floating sensation took over, but instead of rising out of myself as I had last time, I stayed in my body, invisible to everyone else.

"What did you do?" Calrod snarled. "You killed her! I'm going to tear you apart!"

I hated hearing such agony in his voice, but this was the only way.

Carridan released my arm, and I listened to his steps retreat.

"I didn't do this," he argued. "I suppose she wasn't as strong as I believed. Sad, really. I was excited to see what she could do." He sighed and moved further away. The pulsing energy that had come from the circle disappeared, and I chanced lifting my spiritual head up enough to take a look.

I opened my mouth to let out an excited exclamation, but no sound came out, thankfully. Not willing to stay a spirit too long, I fell back into my body. I opened one eye, looking to Morgan. She had tears burning in her eyes and was beating against the barrier. Her hand paused, and she jerked around to look at me, then away again. She went right back to shouting at Carridan, and I let out a quiet breath of relief. She knew I was alive, at least. Now I just had to let Calrod know.

Carridan had migrated toward him and his brothers. He was droning on and on about power and balances and something else I didn't care about. I shifted my head, lifting it enough to find Calrod. Through a sea of legs, I latched onto his face. His eyes shimmered that dark blue. Carridan turned, and Calrod looked right at me. He subtly nodded, and flames sparked at his fingertips. I winked back and prepared myself for what he was about to do. I wouldn't be scared of it this time. Calrod's fire, even its ghost, was as much a part of me as it was of him. I could control it. I could make it do exactly what I needed it to. To save all our lives, I would become what Calrod always said I was. Killing Vanessa had only been the start.

Prince Carridan was going to regret showing his face here.

"I don't have to kill you," Carridan said. "It'd be a shame to waste such power."

"You know what's a real shame?" Calrod replied. "That we only get to kill you once." At his last word, fire exploded from his center, sending it rolling across the ground. Demons shouted and dove out of the way. I half-hoped it'd be enough to kill Carridan, but a shimmering shield appeared around him, probably coming from that damn armband. The fire scorched the trees and the front of Cyrene's house. The demons rushed in, tackling Calrod to the ground, and the flames cut off.

His outburst was more than enough.

I turned my full attention on the ghost of energy Calrod's fire left behind. This time, when my blood burned and my hands warmed, I didn't shy away from the power reaching out to me. I embraced it, drawing it into myself. It was like Calrod stood right beside me, holding my hand. In my mind's eye, I saw the flames building into an inferno, but it wasn't the only energy coursing through my body. The storm's energy I'd used the day I killed Vanessa had stuck around. It enveloped the fire, taking it and twisting it into an entirely new energy that needed to be unleashed.

A rush of power had me standing upright without even realizing I was doing so. My hands flexed, and lightning mixed with fire dripped from my fingertips. I couldn't hold onto it for long, hopefully just long enough.

"She's alive," a demon shouted.

Carridan whipped around, his eyes wide. "You! What are you?"

I held up my hand, not wasting time with words, and sent a blast of lightning and blue fire directly toward him. He held up the arm with the gold band, but the explosion sent him soaring through the air. The swirl of energy didn't stop with him. It went after the demons holding Calrod, Arkon, and Dagon.

Demons scattered, and chaos erupted around us.

I sprinted to Cyrene and pressed my hands to the ground, directly on the glowing circle. The symbols burned to ash, and Cyrene was freed.

"Get the others out and protect Jasmine," she told me, then took off into the fight that had erupted outside her home.

I freed Rik next, then turned my attention to Morgan and Jasmine. Together, we pulled Jasmine as far away from the main fighting as we could, then took up positions in front of her. She was breathing heavily and clutching at her pregnant belly. I exchanged a worried look with Morgan, then returned my attention to the insanity before us. The energy was still alive and well in my veins, and I was going to use every last drop of it while I could.

Rain and wind gusted around me, but they weren't alone. Blue and white embers took to the air, too. I expanded the cocoon to include Morgan and Jasmine. A demon rushed for us, but he was burned and jolted with electricity the moment he made contact. His body fell dead to the ground, and I shrugged.

"Alright, nice to know how that works."

Morgan gave me a wicked grin. "That bracelet," she said, nodding to Carridan, "think you can target it?"

"I can try."

I held up my hands, concentrating on the storm, and thrust it outward while maintaining the shield around the three of us. My vision blurred, but the storm condensed. Fire coated it, and I directed the orb of barely contained raw energy right for Carridan.

13

Calrod

I smashed a demon in the face with my fist, wrapped him in ropes of fire, and tightened. He gasped, his eyes widening. Bones cracked, and he fell to the ground. I stepped over his dead body and moved onto the next target.

Arkon and Dagon fought on either side of me, forming a tight circle. Cyrene and Rik were to our right, cutting a bloody path through the demons. Carridan was behind them, shouting orders. I chanced a look around, inwardly sighing in relief to see Cara had Morgan and Jasmine with her, safe behind the firestorm she'd created. I wanted to yell at her as much as kiss her for the stunt she'd pulled, but damn if she hadn't just saved our asses.

Jasmine let out an ear-piercing scream, and Arkon's bellow answered in kind. We had to end this battle and get her somewhere safe before it was too late. Arkon looked ready to charge in after Carridan, but an orb of swirling energy made me snatch his arm and stop him.

Arkon shouted at me to release him. I forced him to watch as the sphere zeroed in on Carridan and his arm which sported the gold armband. The firestorm condensed then wound around his arm. He cursed, staggering from the force of the attack. The orb exploded, sending him crashing to the ground once more.

The bracelet remained on his arm, but there, running down the side of it, was a crack.

"Enough of this," Carridan bellowed, clambering to his feet. "Get the witches and kill the others!"

We'd taken down a few of his demons but more rushed out of the woods around us. Damn it. How many had he dragged out of the Underworld? They charged, and we met them head-on, fighting our way closer to Cara, Morgan, and Jasmine. A line of demons to my right was taken down by a tidal wave of thorn-covered vines that dragged them into the forest. I assumed it was courtesy of Cyrene.

I ducked under the dagger of a charging demon and shoved my fist into his gut. He gasped, and I grabbed him by the head, snapping his neck. The storm Cara had been using to protect them was fading fast. Several demons closed in on them. I charged forward, straining to get to them in time.

Three demons rushed me, and I was driven back. The storm fell, and I shouted my rage to the sky. Cara and Morgan fell back, keeping Jasmine behind them. I wasn't going to get there in time.

Jasmine screamed again, and the air in front of the women burst to life with red and orange embers. Was Cara doing that somehow? From the confused glance she gave Morgan, she wasn't.

Jasmine shrieked even louder, and the embers took on the form of a dragon towering over the demons. It threw back its head with a vicious roar that shook the ground and chased the birds from nearby trees. The beast stomped toward the demons and they took off running. The dragon spread two massive wings, blocking Cara and the others from sight. I had no idea how there was a dragon here but didn't stop to question it.

Carridan's demons were fleeing. This was our chance to stop him, and I wasn't about to waste it. I exchanged a look with Dagon and Arkon, then the three of us stalked toward him. We killed the few demons who got in our way to try and stop us, then it was the prince and us.

"You will never defeat me," Carridan warned. The bracelet sparked with power. "You hear me? Never! I will have what I came for."

My lip twitched, and fire coated my hands. I charged in first, aiming for the bracelet. A burst of air pushed me back, but Arkon and Dagon were right there to sprint in next. Vines launched out of the ground, winding around Carridan's legs to try and hold him in place. Rik latched himself onto Carridan's back, but a bright, gold flash knocked us all back once again. Two swords of golden flames appeared in Carridan's hands. He waved us forward, his gaze filled with madness.

The demons who hadn't fled turned their attention to us. The dragon had disappeared, but no one was going after Cara and the others for the moment. She and Morgan were crouched beside Jasmine. I wanted to shout for Arkon to go to her, but Carridan shoved the tips of the swords into the ground. It cracked and split open, threatening to swallow us. We stumbled to get away. Darkness spewed from the earth like a fog, cutting off my vision. Grunts of pain sounded around me. A body flew past my right, and another slammed right into me.

I raised my fist, but it was Arkon. We hauled each other up and pressed our backs together.

"We have to get out of this shit," he muttered.

"Your magic work?"

"Nothing," he snapped. "The fog's putting a damper on it. What about fire?"

I waited for flames to appear in my hand, but the fog collapsed around them, snuffing them out. We were running out of options. A familiar yell came from our left, and we moved closer, bumping into a body on the ground. I grabbed Dagon's hand and yanked him upright. He looked about as good as the rest of us did, covered in blood and dirt. We remained in a circle, our backs together. I peered through the fog, willing it to clear. The wind gusted, and leaves swirled around us. A tugging started in my gut. With a curse, I was thrown into the air, Arkon and Dagon with me. By the time we hit the ground, landing on our asses, the fog was blown away.

Cyrene. It had to be her. I spun around, seeing her surrounded by more gusting winds and green leaves, fighting Carridan alone. He was down to one blade, but the bracelet remained on his wrist. Violet light cracked at her fingertips, and she shoved her hand into the ground. Vines erupted, winding around Carridan's body and pinning his arms to his sides. The second sword went out, and I held my breath, waiting for her to finish him off. The vines crushed his body and his face twisted in agony.

The bracelet glowed, the rubies exploding, and gold light swallowed Carridan and Cyrene. I yelled for her to get out of there, but she refused to move. I was going to rush in, but Rik was faster. He disappeared into the light, and a heartbeat later, a blast sent us flying into the front of the house.

I grunted from the impact, falling forward to all fours. Arkon and Dagon groaned next to me, alive for the moment. I quickly scanned the area for Cara. The explosion hadn't seemed to reach her, thank the gods.

"I grow tired of this game," Carridan snapped, the gold light fading. "I had plans for you, witch, but now I see you're better off dead!"

Cyrene was on the ground, with Rik before her. I

stumbled toward them, not about to watch Carridan kill anyone else. He threw his hand to the right, and I was hurled right back into the house. Cyrene was yelling at Rik to run, but he stood his ground, hissing at Carridan.

"You should've listened to her." Carridan blocked Rik's first hit and headbutted him. He wound his hand around Rik's neck, lifting him off his feet.

Cyrene shouted, pushing herself upright, but it was too late. Another golden sword appeared in Carridan's hand, and he drove it through Rik's chest.

"No!" Cyrene screamed, dragging herself forward.

Rik's eyes widened, then narrowed while a smile stretched his lips. I wasn't sure why he was grinning like that until I noticed where his hand was. He'd closed it around Carridan's arm and the bracelet. The tattoos that usually danced on his arms had slithered down to cover the magical artifact. Rik opened his hand, and the armband shattered like glass. The blade vanished, and Rik hit the grass, his eyes void of life.

Cyrene reached him, holding his head in her lap. My heart ached for her, but there would be time to mourn later.

Carridan was staring at his bare arm in disbelief. "No," he whispered, shaking his head and muttering the word over and over. "You— What did you do? What did you do to me?"

Arkon drew Soul Piercer from the sheath at his hip, and I readied my fire. Dagon flipped his two daggers over, nodding to us. Together, we moved in for the kill. Carridan's head jerked up at our approach. He raised his hand, but there was no magic left in him. He was nothing but a demon.

"Protect me," he shouted to the few demons left alive. "Save me!"

"No one will save you now," Cyrene whispered.

She hadn't gotten to her feet, but she didn't have to. Eyes glowing red, she held her hand out to the forest. The ground shook, and branches rustled. I expected more vines to appear. Instead, I was greeted by the sight of three large oak trees rising from the dirt and marching toward the demons. Their branches and roots launched out, snatching the devils the second they turned to run. Their dying screams faded away, and Carridan paled.

"Wait," he pleaded, holding out his hands to us. "Just wait. I'm a prince. You can't simply execute me."

"Oh, I think we can," I said. "You see, you're in our world now."

"You made a mistake when you came after our family," Dagon added, closing in on his right.

"And now, you're going to pay for that mistake in kind." Arkon gripped Soul Piercer hard in his fist, his lips peeling back from his fangs.

Carridan gulped, then threw himself forward, trying to run. My fire latched around him and yanked him right back. Dagon shoved him to his knees and placed a dagger at his throat. While we held Carridan in place, Arkon moved in.

"It won't matter," Carridan whispered. "None of this will. You can't stop it. No one can. Killing me will solve nothing, you hear me? Nothing. The darkness will still come for you, for all of you."

"So be it," Arkon whispered, drew his arm back, and plunged the dagger into Carridan's chest. His body exploded, dousing us in gore. What remained of him hit the ground between us.

Dead. Carridan was finally dead. The rush of relief at seeing his corpse was quickly overshadowed by Cara's panicked yell.

"Arkon! Jasmine could really use you right now."

He dropped the dagger and hurried to Jasmine's side. He tried to move her, but Jasmine shook her head, grabbing for his arm. "We need to get you inside."

"No. I can't move. Not now," she rasped. "Our baby's coming right now."

Morgan was perched between Jasmine's legs. "Uh, yeah, she's not lying. There's no time. Cyrene! I could use your help."

Worried Cyrene wasn't going to be able to help, I was going to tell Morgan we had to go to Plan B. Then the witch breezed by me and took Morgan's place. Dagon and I joined the rest of them, him hauling Morgan into his arms and me doing the same to Cara. She appeared ready to pass out, and slumped into my side.

There were too many things I wanted to say to her but now wasn't the time. Jasmine screamed, and Arkon cursed while she dug her nails into his arm. He shifted closer, helping prop her up, then Cyrene was telling her to push. Arkon looked beyond panicked. He kissed Jasmine's temple, telling her she could do it. I winced, feeling for her while she struggled through the labor of bringing their kid into the world. She sagged, and Cyrene told her to rest for a moment.

"I think, I think I made that dragon," Jasmine murmured. "Pretty cool, huh?"

Arkon grinned, shaking his head. "Yeah, pretty cool. You're incredible, you know that?"

Jasmine smiled for a second, then she was yelling again, and Cyrene was telling her to push one last time. A baby's cry came moments later, and I stilled, not believing this was happening today of all days.

"Your little girl is going to be just fine," Cyrene assured Jasmine, resting the newborn baby on her chest.

My chest grew tight, and I swiped at my eyes. Cara had tears running down her cheeks. She clung to me, and for the first time, I could see us having a family of our own. One day, maybe. Carridan was dead, but his words about darkness coming lingered in my mind.

Dagon and Morgan helped Arkon, and Jasmine get inside with their baby. Cyrene had drifted back to Rik's dead body. Cara and I walked to her, neither of us seeming to want to leave her alone in her grief.

"I'm sorry," Cara whispered.

Cyrene smiled sadly, running her fingers down Rik's cheek. She kissed his forehead, then folded his hands over his chest. "Death comes for us all," she replied quietly. "Today is a day for me to mourn, but not you. I'll be alright out here. I need to give Rik a proper send-off. You two need to be with your family. I'll see to the rest of the dead demons, too."

"Cyrene," I said, but she gave me a pleading look. There were still questions I had that needed answers, mostly about Carridan and her and why he'd been so intent on killing Rik. They could wait. They'd have to. "Yell if you need us," I told her, and with Cara's hand in mine, we followed the others into the house.

We barely made it over the threshold when Cara collapsed. I scooped her into my arms, immediately surrounding her with my fire.

"Hmm, that feels nice," she murmured, her eyes closed. She snuggled into my chest, and I sighed. "What was that for?"

"You being you."

"Hey, me being me saved our asses."

I grunted, not wanting to argue. Watching her collapse like that after Carridan touched her, I'd feared the worst. Then I'd seen her spirit form rise for just a second. She was right. She'd been more than ready to stand against Carridan. The firestorm she created was no easy feat of magic. I was going to tell her until I heard her steady breathing.

"Cara?"

"Hmm?" she asked sleepily, curling even more into my chest.

I leaned over, pressing my lips to her forehead. "Never mind, love. Never mind." I carried her upstairs, passing Dagon and Morgan on my way. They were giggling, pulling each other into their bedroom, and shutting the door. Arkon and Jasmine were talking quietly, their voices drifting into the hall, but I let them be. They deserved some time alone with their new baby. I took Cara to our room, laid her down on the bed, and joined her. I hadn't planned on falling asleep, figuring I'd go check on Cyrene, but the second my head hit the pillow and Cara pressed herself against me, exhaustion took hold.

We'd survived today. Carridan was dead. Jasmine and Arkon's baby was safe. We'd lost Rik, but somehow, I had a feeling that was always going to be his destiny. I wrapped my arms around Cara, holding her as close as I could. Maybe now, for a few weeks at least, we'd simply get to live our lives. I ran my fingers over the burn Carridan left on her arm. I had no idea what that symbol meant and almost wished I never would. That it meant nothing at all, and Cara was indeed safe.

Then there was the concern of what the other princes would do once they learned of Carridan's fate. This might very well be the last peaceful night we had together. Or we'd get lucky, and no one would find out what happened to the late prince.

If only that were true. If only I could believe it was possible that fate wasn't about to send us for a ride all over again.

14

Cara

Little baby Zoe fussed, and Jasmine rocked her gently to calm her back down. Mother and daughter had returned to the farmhouse a few days after the fight at Cyrene's place. Arkon had ensured their home was more than ready for them to be where they should've been all along. Not that any of us were too worried about Jasmine being able to defend herself now. According to Cyrene, the dragon she'd manifested was part of her ability to create illusions. I was curious as to what else she could conjure, but a dragon was guaranteed to scare off anyone idiotic enough to come after her.

Jasmine sat on the couch and held out her hand

to Arkon. "Come here for a second. I have to pee," she told him.

I chuckled while Arkon gulped and crossed the room to where Jasmine sat. Calrod was grinning from beside me. Dagon and Morgan stood in the doorway to the kitchen, talking quietly. She squeezed his hand, and his eyes lit up. Whatever Morgan told him had his arm slipping around her waist and kissing her temple.

"She's so damn tiny," Arkon whispered.

"Yeah, she is. Here you go." Jasmine handed Zoe over to Arkon, patted him on the shoulder, and walked down the hall.

Arkon's eyes were wide while he watched his daughter squirming in his arms and start crying. Panic appeared on his face, but he rocked her, cradling her to his chest, and hummed just as Jasmine always did. Though his humming was in tune. Zoe reached up toward his face, and her laughter turned to cooing. I glanced toward the hall, catching Jasmine standing at the end of it, peeking around the corner. She swiped at her eyes, then darted out of sight.

"I have a kid," Arkon murmured after Zoe had fallen asleep.

"Yeah, you do," Calrod said and patted him lightly on the shoulder. "Don't fuck this up, eh?"

"Don't plan on it," Arkon replied, his eyes never leaving Zoe. "She's going to have horns. Look."

We all moved closer to take a gander at Zoe's head. Beneath the bit of peach fuzz hair were two dark spots. They looked rough to the touch already. When tiny sparks ignited at her fingertips, Arkon burst out laughing.

"My little magic user," he whispered and sweetly kissed the top of her head. "Nothing bad will ever happen to you or your momma. Swear it."

I shifted closer to Calrod, glancing up to see his eyes shimmering a dark blue. He hugged me to him, grinning down at me. I'd never thought of kids before. They'd never been on my radar. Now, though, now I began to wonder what it'd be like to see Calrod holding his own kid. I turned, searching for the other visitor who'd stopped by today, but she wasn't inside. Morgan caught my eye and nodded toward the front door. I slipped away from Calrod and stepped onto the porch.

"Cyrene?"

She leaned on the porch railing wearing one of her usual flowing dresses. The green hue was the same shade as Rik's skin. Her violet hair wasn't as vibrant, but I wasn't surprised. She offered me a half-smile then went back to gazing toward the forest.

"I'm sorry," I said, standing beside her. "I know that doesn't do much, but we're all sorry. Can we do anything?"

"No," she sighed. "I'm afraid this is something I have to face on my own." Vines grew out from under her hands, the flowers were a melancholy shade of blue. "His death was fated as much as I wanted to believe it wasn't."

"What do you mean?"

"Many years ago, I saw it, saw him die. I never knew when or by whose hand, but I knew one day the fae I'd come to love would be killed protecting me." Her quiet laughter was weighted down by sorrow that spoke to my soul.

If Calrod had been killed, I wouldn't have been handling it so well.

"I saw it so long ago," she went on, "I'd let myself believe it wouldn't come to pass. Stubborn fae. I even tried to get him to leave, even before that horrible day. He always refused. Said I needed him too much."

"He loved you," I said with a shrug. "It's what we do for those we love. Stay by them."

Cyrene's face became set, and her eyes flared, but

the color was off, almost sickly in hue. "Yes, something I will make sure will never happen again. You can count on that."

I wanted to ask what she meant, but a car pulled up the drive toward the house. The warding Arkon had replaced sparked to life, and the vehicle was forced to stop outside it. If they'd been human, it would've let them through.

I tensed, already pulling on the firestorm that dwelled within me. Calrod, Dagon, and Morgan rushed out the door behind me. The car doors opened, and two men stepped out of their vehicles. They glanced around, but whatever they said, I was too far away to hear.

Calrod growled and charged down the steps, Dagon on his heels. "Princes," he snapped.

"What?" I blurted.

Arkon barreled out of the house next, his face set in a furious scowl. Jasmine had Zoe in her arms, but gold and amber magic swirled in her eyes. She raised her hand, and a burst of reddish-orange light shot from her body, zooming to where the two demons stood. Their glamour stayed intact until a dragon morphed into being and roared viciously in their direction. Morgan, Cyrene, and I took up defensive positions in front of the house, bracing for a fight.

"Wait!" The demons were waving their arms over their heads. "We're here to talk!"

Calrod, Dagon, and Arkon stormed down the gravel drive to where the dragon illusion kept the princes at bay. Jasmine didn't let it disappear until Arkon waved his hand over his head at her. Her lips thinned, but she released the illusion. The dragon grunted, voicing her disagreement with Arkon, then vanished as shimmering trails of red and orange light carried away with the breeze.

"Who are they?" I asked Cyrene.

Vines had sprouted beneath her feet at the sight of the princes. She stepped to the edge of the porch, breaking the twisting brambles and creating new ones. The two men had dropped their glamours, their horns glinting in the late afternoon sun.

"Cousins," she finally replied. "Looks as if you get to meet more of the family."

"Cousins?" I asked. "I didn't know they had any family left."

Calrod held out his arm to the demon on the right, and they embraced. I exchanged a look with Morgan and Jasmine, glad to see I wasn't the only one suspicious of them showing up here a few days after we offed Carridan. The brothers approached, the princes with them, and Calrod motioned toward the porch.

"Cara, Morgan, Cyrene, and Jasmine, these are our cousins." Calrod pointed to the demon with the reddish tint to his horns first, then the slightly shorter one with utterly black horns. His eyes were so dark brown, they too appeared black. "Prince Aithen and his brother Prince Tazarek."

None of us responded, and the tension in the air visibly crackled.

"They're not here to fight," Arkon said, looking right at Jasmine.

"Then why are they here?" she demanded. "Why show up now? What do they want?"

The princes exchanged a glance, then Aithen, the one with the reddish-hued horns, stepped forward. He placed a hand to his heart and bowed. "We would've come sooner if we were able. I'm afraid we had no idea our cousins lived until a couple of days ago. When we were alerted to what Carridan had done, we sought them out."

"Why?" I snapped this time, the firestorm inside me ready to be unleashed if need be.

"You have nothing to fear from the other princes or us," Aithen assured, his words punctuated with a growl. "Carridan's death was beyond justified."

"There's much to discuss," Tazarek added, his voice far deeper than his cousin's. "Carridan betrayed the princes of the Underworld. Somehow, he kept us in a daze these last few decades."

"All of you? How?" Morgan asked this time.

Aithen's lips curled, and he looked to Dagon and the others. "You have certainly found fearsome mates on the surface."

"You have no idea," Dagon said, grinning.

"Be that as it may, Carridan has left a mess in the Underworld. We have come to ask the three of you return to take up your rightful places there and to rule as you should've been doing all this time," Aithen said.

"No," the brothers said simultaneously.

Aithen's brow furrowed, and Tazarek's expression turned to one of confusion. "Why not?" he asked.

Calrod reached for my hand, and I went to stand beside him. "Because this is our home now. We're not leaving it."

"You don't understand. What we've found in Carridan's palace, what he's been doing for years, it's beyond comprehension. I'm afraid the trouble he started is far from over. Many of his demons have fled. We need help tracking them down," Aithen explained in a rush. "Then there are the victims we found in his dungeons." He grunted in disgust. "I have no way to explain what I saw down there. Please, cousins, I know you've been through a living hell, and we have no right to ask for your aid, but here we are doing just that."

Arkon, Dagon, and Calrod exchanged a look I knew meant they were going to help. As much as I wanted to argue, Carridan's dying words stuck with me. He'd said this wasn't over. And he hadn't merely come to the surface to kill the brothers.

He'd come for Cyrene and us. He'd come for Jasmine and Arkon's baby.

"Cara?" Calrod asked. "If you tell me no, I'll listen to you. What we're getting into, I have no way to know how dangerous it might be."

I shifted my gaze to Morgan and Jasmine. The three of us had been through so much shit in the last year. I wanted to say it had been enough danger and fear to last me a lifetime, but Cyrene had hinted time and again she'd come looking for us for a reason. Whatever purpose we had for finding our demon mates and being here together in this moment, it wasn't over. If we said no and turned our backs on the princes, the plans Carridan might've already set in motion would find a way to catch up with us. That's what my gut told me. Morgan and Jasmine nodded, and I, in turn, did the same to Calrod.

"I'm with you," I told him. "Sounds like it's going to be a very long evening."

"Understatement of the year," Jasmine muttered. "Alright, everyone inside. One wrong move and I'll make you both wish you'd stayed in the Underworld," she warned the princes. Arkon rolled his eyes, following her back inside.

The others followed, but Cyrene hadn't moved from her place on the porch. I told Calrod I'd be there in a minute and went to her. The sorrow that had been in her eyes was gone, replaced with a calculating look I wasn't sure I liked.

"You know what they're talking about, don't you," I said quietly. "Carridan's plans."

"As you said," she replied, "it's going to be a long night." She stormed inside the house, the screen door slamming behind her.

"Damn," I whispered, hating how the sickening sensation in my gut kept growing.

The symbol Carridan had burned into my left forearm gave a twinge. I covered it with my hand, wondering if we'd ever be able to remove it or if that mark just sealed all our fates in Carridan's game.

Cyrene had told us she had an idea of what the symbol represented but needed to consult the Witches Archives before giving us a definite answer. She was headed there in the morning. My gut told me I already knew the mark was terrible news for all of us.

"Cara?"

I spun around and hugged Calrod, wanting to assure myself he was still here with me. He kissed the top of my head, holding me until I looked up at him.

"What's wrong?" he asked.

"I don't know, but I wish I did."

A worried growl rumbled through his chest, but I stood on my toes and kissed him. I wanted to stay out on that porch for hours. Wanted nothing more than to take his hand and go back to my place, pretend his cousins hadn't shown up. But they had. The fight wasn't over as we'd hoped. I memorized Calrod's face in the light of the setting sun. He seemed to do the same to me, trailing his fingers along the curve of my face then under my chin. His lips brushed softly against mine, then we were clutching each other like this was going to be our last night together.

Neither of us said anything. We'd never have to. We let out a deep breath together, and hand in hand, went inside to see what else destiny had in store for all of us.

AFTERWORD

Click for more Ava Benton works!

Sign up for the newsletter to be notified of new releases.

Click on link for
Newsletter
or put this in your browser window:
mailerlite.com/webforms/landing/m7a8c5

www.ingramcontent.com/pod-product-compliance
Lightning Source LLC
Chambersburg PA
CBHW020316160726
47992CB00004B/1555